Committing

The first novel by

Benjamin Wood

FOR YOU,
WHOEVER YOU MAY BE

ACKNOWLEDGMENTS

Thank you first and foremost to Chelsey Gensel, Erin Anthony, Kassidee Lank, David Willis and Katie Fredrickson for reviewing the early drafts of this novel. I asked each of them to stop me before I embarrassed myself, so you have their consenting approval to blame for the words you are about to read.

Thank you Erin Jacobs and J.P. Allen for your help with the cover. I may or may not be able to write but I definitely have no eye for design.

A special thank you to my sister Mandie for her support and encouragement.

I'd also like to thank my friends, who inspired many of the characters in these pages.
You inspire me still.

PART I
Leap

CHAPTER ONE

There is a beautiful library in downtown Salt Lake City. It is made up of two seemingly separate structures: the first, a glass tear drop, four stories tall, housing rows of books, computers, and conference rooms; the second, a sweeping arm topped by a sloped stairway that rises from the plaza outside to the roof of the main building.

The two structures are, of course, connected, but within the library's glass walls they are divided by an atrium with café tables and used books for sale where musicians occasionally perform. The arm contains a row of study tables on each level, offering a quiet space for reading and studying. From there, you can look across the empty space to the organized sea of volumes and tomes that lie beyond.

It was there, on a Saturday morning, that Charles was sitting – the top floor of the Salt Lake City Library. His

1

elbows were rested on the table in front of him, causing his body to pitch forward in the kind of youthful slouch that would have prompted his mother to swoop in and straighten him in his younger years. He was staring into the dull glow of a computer screen, his head weighed down further by a chord connected to the headphones that tethered him to where he sat.

The video he was watching ended and slowly he closed his laptop and cast his gaze across the void to his right at a mother and two small children climbing a curved staircase to the third floor. Gathering his things, he began walking back across the atrium to the other side and stopped on the breezeway that connects the two sections. From where he stood he hovered in the air directly above the library's main entrance and as he peered over the breezeway's edge at the atrium floor some 80 feet below he allowed his weight to carry him over, and down. The cool air licked at his face, forcing his eyes closed as he fell, weightless and free, to the floor.

But it wasn't real.

Charles remained sitting in front of his laptop, his headphones over his ears playing an instrumental soundtrack as credits panned up the screen in front of him. In his mind he could hear the dull thud as his body struck the floor below. There was a swath of light pouring in through the windows where his body would land and he wondered if somehow, even though his soul – if there was such a thing – was slipping away, he would feel the warmth on his skin.

There were about a dozen individuals meandering just outside the doors, not to mention the countless people within the library's walls. Among them, as always, was no small number of derelicts, offensive to all five senses and taking advantage of a quiet space to sit and spend the day near public restrooms. Charles often thought how it made for an odd combination, as the public library always seemed to be evenly split between khakhi-shorts-wearing children and their parents, hipster bookworms and homeless, drug-addicted lowlifes. *Then again*, Charles' mind always seemed to say, *where would you go if you had nowhere to go? It makes more sense than the mall.*

There would be an immediate panic. A piercing scream would echo through the vast, silent space, bouncing off of glass, concrete and paper. The confusion would not last long. Officers patrolling the grounds would respond immediately, call for an ambulance and begin diverting the rubbernecking public from the area. His body would be removed, covered in a plastic sheet and wheeled off to some forgotten and seldom-seen corner of the city where suicide victims were taken prior to being released to their families. The floor would be cleaned and by the next morning, at the latest, the library would open its doors and greet the public.

What would they use? Charles thought. *A mop? A broom? A shovel?*

For his family, of course, the emotional clean-up would not be so swift and it was the arrival of that thought, the sense of pain that his death could cause to others, that finally broke Charles from the macabre fantasy. The music in his ears had stopped and the website was asking him if he wanted to continue on to the next episode. On the screen was the frozen image of some busty brunette, a promise of the kind of zany, escapist shenanigans you can only get from a television sitcom.

The mother and her children reached the top of the stairs. Upon seeing a full row of nothing but gleaming comic books the boy, probably 10 or 11, darted off and begun pulling volume after volume from the rack with a face of pure, ecstatic joy while several issues spilled to the floor.

Charles closed his laptop. Gathering his things, he passed over the breezeway, pausing briefly at the center only to enjoy the sudden beat of sunlight at his back and then, with a breath, he continued on to the other side, down the stairs, and out the lobby doors below.

It begins at a funeral.

Stories like this one always seem to start with some catalyst, like a birth or a wedding. As it happened, this one begins with a death.

After more than six years, Devin Wallace had lost his valiant battle with leukemia. Charles met him in 2006. By some twist of fate they had been assigned each other as dormitory roommates. They had no way of knowing then that in a matter of months Devin would be diagnosed.

For most of their friendship his disease was simply a part of him. It defined him. He was Devin, "the one with cancer." He had beaten it before and he would surely do it again.

Except he didn't.

So Charles biked through the dirty sludge of a fading winter back to his one-bedroom apartment and changed into a black suit. He slipped on his black shoes, which he had shined the night before, over his black socks. He fed a black belt through black beltloops and fastened the silver buckle. He buttoned up the collar of his white shirt and stood before the mirror as he fixed a narrow black tie.

The tie's slim cut, he thought, was a little *Friday night* for a funeral but it was the only black tie that he had. His others were all of the bright, solid color variety – "power" ties in commanding reds, purples and greens –

which obviously wouldn't do. As he looked at his reflection he wasn't sure if he looked too somber, or not somber enough. He looked good, he thought, but then thought that he ought not try to look good, which immediately gave way to the thought that he certainly ought not to not look good.

Devin was 26. They both were, technically speaking, except Devin was dead. Charles would turn 27 in three months but in photographs, old videos and memories Devin would stay perpetually 26 for as long as Charles lived. Longer, actually, since as long as there were people still living who remembered Devin alive he would continually be Mr. Devin Wallace, deceased March 2, 2013 at age 26. Charles could die tomorrow, he reminded himself, and that would have no effect on when Devin had finally succumbed to the disease inside his blood.

But what about when everyone who once knew Devin was dead? How old would he be then, when every trace of him was erased from the earth and everyone who had ever held a lingering knowledge of his existence was gone? At that point Devin would not be 26, Charles thought, he would be nothing at all.

Devin was also married. He and Stephanie Elizabeth Wallace, maiden name Christensen, had been legally and lawfully wedded on October 4, 2008 after dating for just under two years in college. Much like the cancer, Charles had met Devin shortly before Devin met Stephanie, and so she had come to define him as well. Charles' best friend Devin, the one with cancer, Stephanie's boyfriend/fiancé/husband and now Mr. Devin Wallace, deceased March 2, 2013 at age 26.

Their son, Daniel, was born February 24, 2010. Devin's cancer came soaring out of remission the month after Stephanie got pregnant. It had always been a possibility, one that they had accepted and planned for as best as possible. Every milestone was an event, checked off an imaginary list like a game show contestant scrambling to win a prize before the buzzer rang.

Devin won many prizes. He saw his son's first steps, he heard his first word. He helped his wife with the potty training, took a photograph of his son on Santa's lap and lived long enough to see Daniel turn three years old. Charles knew how happy that had made Devin.

He scooped up his keys and wallet on his way out the door. Locking his apartment behind him, he started making his way down the cold, echoing stairwell, arriving one level down before the door to his floor swung shut with a reverberating boom that rippled down the walls like the sliding bars in a prison. For whatever reason, Charles suddenly became fixated on the idea that he was alone in a concrete cylinder that stretched six flights above the ground and two flights beneath it. In his mind he stripped away the walls, floors and ceilings that surrounded him and instead imagined himself floating, 20 feet in the air, standing tall and rigid in a black suit and skinny tie.

Charles bounded down the remaining flights to his car in the basement parking lot, arriving slightly out of breath. It had been a few days since he had driven last and when he turned the ignition the car sputtered slightly in the cold before the speakers blared to life, blasting him back against his seat with the sound of a rousing instrumental chorus from whatever CD he had been listening to. He quickly reached out and shut it off, plunging the space into abject silence.

He sat there for a moment, staring forward into the empty parking stalls in front of him. His fingers where white, the blood having left them at the request of his awkwardly tight grip on the wheel. Glancing up he saw his reflection in the rear-view mirror and straightened his tie.

Charles turned the volume down on his stereo and pushed play. As the music began he shifted his car into drive and inched slowly forward, and out.

CHAPTER TWO

The church was beautiful, a display of minimalist perfection with only a few muted white blossoms and black and white photographs drawing attention away from the ornate structure and its elaborate stained-glass windows. As he entered, Charles couldn't help but think how lucky Devin was to have married Stephanie, and how lucky Stephanie was that Devin would never plan her funeral. Charles was no more than two steps through the door when little Daniel bounded up to him and wrapped himself around Charles' leg. He always greeted him this way. Charles called it his Daniel-Socks and would walk around with the young boy sitting on his foot, arms and legs firmly secured behind his calf.

"Uncle Charles!"

"Hey Dan," Charles said, reaching down and tussling

the boy's head. Stephanie arrived immediately and bent down to smooth her son's hair back into place before rising to give Charles a hug.

"Steph, this is beautiful."

"Thanks Charles," she said before directing her attention to her son. "Come on Dan, Uncle Charles needs to go sit down."

"I can take him with me, if you want. What do you say Dan-Socks? Want to sit with me and Uncle Tyler?" Charles said, noticing the small line of arriving guests waiting to give their condolences to Stephanie. She merely nodded and mouthed the words "thank you" before turning to embrace a large woman, trembling visibly between unsuccessfully muted sobs.

"Hold on buddy," Charles said, feeling Daniel's grip tighten around his leg in response.

He walked with a dogged gait, making a louder stomp each time his loaded right shoe struck the floor. He wondered what malady people must assume had befallen him if they were sitting more than 10 feet away and were therefore unaware of the 30 pounds of three-year-old attached to his pants. Tyler was sitting six rows from the front and was watching him arrive, having turned like everyone else to see who was making all the noise.

"Hey Dude," Tyler said, sliding over to allow room.

Tyler was a large man, the kind that you assume had attended some junior college on a football scholarship. In actuality, he was an engineer or something. Charles wasn't entirely sure what Tyler did for a living besides get paid more than he deserved.

"Where's Trish?" Charles asked, peeling Daniel off and setting him down on the bench beside him.

"Work. She'll be here later."

Trish and Tyler made up the third branch of their little family. Tyler had lived down the hall from the dorm room Charles and Devin shared their freshman year. He had dated Trish in high school when he was a senior and she was a doe-eyed idiot of a sophomore cheerleader.

When she finally graduated, she conveniently enrolled in the same university they attended, poised to win back her man. After four years of unrelenting affection – during which Trish was a constant presence in all of their lives despite Tyler's insistence that they were not, nor would ever be, in a relationship – he had finally succumbed to reality and proposed.

"How are the plans going?" Charles asked.

"Well, my criteria for 'success' is not being bankrupt after the honeymoon," Tyler said. "And in that sense, it's not going well."

"Isn't her dad supposed to pay for everything? That's

a thing, right? Father of the bride and all that?"

"Her dad's a stingy bastard and she's a feminist," Tyler said, "which apparently means she wants the wedding she feels she deserves, paid for with her own money, which really means she wants the wedding of her dreams paid for with *my* money."

"All's fair."

"Is it?"

Someone that Charles should have remembered walked by and gave both him and Tyler a handshake, the kind where the person clasps you with two hands, over and under simultaneously. The woman, probably in her late 50s with slightly graying hair, gave each of them their own individual two-minute session of hand-swallowing and fixed, compassionate eye contact. She said nothing, apparently confident that her condolences were being adequately transmitted either telepathically or through touch.

For their part, Charles and Tyler both put on an appropriately sympathetic and affectionate smile and nodded in that way people do at solemn occasions.

"Who was that?" Charles asked.

"No idea," Tyler replied. "So Trish is mad at me, we kind of had a fight this morning."

"What about?"

"Well, she was on my case about not caring about some dumb wedding detail, centerpieces or something, and then all the sudden she says 'if you hadn't waited so long to propose then maybe Devin would have been at the wedding.' Can you believe that Shit?"

Charles wasn't looking at his friend and didn't respond immediately. His attention was focused on Daniel who was struggling to un-tuck his little white dress shirt from the waist of his pants. "That's messed up," he said finally.

Tyler looked to see what Charles was watching and fixed his eyes on Daniel, who had succeeded with his shirt and was now fumbling with cherubic fingers to loosen the bow tie that had become twisted and tight around his neck. Tyler turned back towards the front of the chapel. "Yeah man," he said softly. "It's messed up."

Charles scanned the room. He could see Devin's parents toward the front of the chapel, sitting hand in hand with rigid backs. As if sensing Charles' gaze, Devin's mother turned and met his eyes with an affectionate smile, dipped her head slightly and then turned back toward the casket that was placed directly in front of her.

It was large, even for a casket, but was otherwise unimposing. The lacquered chestnut was broken only by the silver handle that ran along the side. For the most part, it blended in with the dais at the front of the chapel.

Charles didn't recognize many of the other guests. He swept his head in one last 180-degree pass from side to side, touching briefly on a few cousins or family friends that he thought he recognized from encounters over the years. Just as his view returned to the front of the room he felt Tyler's elbow jab his ribs.

"Oh man!" Tyler said in an excited whisper, "Back door, right side. Look who just walked in."

He put his arm on the bench behind Tyler to better turn himself and froze when he saw her. Blond hair that fell between her shoulder blades. A sleeveless black dress that stopped just above the knee, giving way to two flawless legs held in perfect shape by a pair of striking heels.

Jessica.

"I didn't know she was back in town," Tyler said. "How long has it been since you saw her. Three, four years?"

"Five," Charles said, his eyes still fixed on her as she passed behind the pews toward Stephanie. She moved effortlessly, the kind of woman who was born in heels and confident in any setting. It wasn't so much a step as it was a sort of gliding motion across the floor, like a the bow of a ship piercing through ocean waves. In every way she looked like she had just walked across the street from where she was filming a Maybelline commercial.

"You gotta talk to her after, get her number," Tyler said. "Damn, can you believe how good she looks?"

"Dude, I hardly think it's appropriate to pick up chicks at Devin's funeral," Charles replied, louder than he intended. He quickly ducked his head down, hunkering into the pew like a frightened turtle. He could feel his pulse on the left side of his neck.

"Are you kidding me?" Tyler said, oblivious to any sense of volume decorum. "You know Devin would be proud if his funeral helped you get back together with Jessica Warner."

"Just…shut up man."

"I think she's here alone, I'll wave her over," Tyler said, rising halfway out of his seat before Charles forcefully grabbed his arm and pulled him back down.

"Dude, they're starting," Charles said. Tyler looked embarrassed and quickly composed himself as the pastor took to the pulpit and invited everyone to take their seats. From the corner of his eye Charles watched Jessica move into a pew by herself near the door. His attention was snapped back forward when Stephanie began addressing the guests.

"Thank you all so much for coming," she began.

"You may not have known this, but Devin hated hosting parties. He told me once that in high school he had tried to put something together last minute on Halloween. There was a single bag of chips on the kitchen table, about a dozen guys taking turns playing foosball and one girl, just one, sitting sullenly in the corner. He was so shamed and scarred by the experience that he vowed to never host anything for the rest of his life. If I ever approached the subject he would throw one fist to the sky and scream 'Never Again!'"

She paused for a moment and pressed her hand to her mouth, her eyes wet with suppressed tears.

"When his condition worsened, we knew that certain preparations had to be taken care of. He wrote his will and something like 40 letters for my son, Daniel, to open on specific birthdays. I have them at home, in a box tucked away in our closet. He said that it was important that a boy learn certain things from his father and it took him about two weeks to decide at what age Daniel should get the sex talk."

Charles put an arm around Daniel and scooted him close to his hip. The boy was completely naïve to everything being said but was frantically waving at his mother, trying to draw her attention. Stephanie looked down and saw him and broke into a wide, tearful smile.

"Hi Daniel," she said. "I'm glad you're listening because you're going to get an awkward letter from daddy in 11 years."

Everyone laughed as Stephanie stood there, beaming with glistening eyes.

"Whenever the funeral came up, Devin would just stop the conversation. I remember one night he said to me 'Babe, you know what the silver lining in this is? It's my party, but I won't have to plan any of it and if no one shows up, well, I'm dead anyway.'"

Stephanie didn't talk much longer. She retold the story of meeting Devin, how his diagnosis had arrived like a lightning bolt just as things where starting to get serious between them. She told how they both decided they weren't ready to give up on each other and that come what may, they would face it together.

And that was it. She stopped abruptly, which led Charles to believe that she had prepared more to say, and walked down into the audience to sit by her mother, who pulled her daughter in tight and set her head down on her shoulder. After Stephanie, Devin's mother spoke, then his father and then the pastor gave a few last words.

Charles stood, holding Daniel, and walked to the front of the chapel with Tyler close behind. He handed Daniel to his mother then turned, joined by the other pallbearers, and lifted the casket up over his shoulder. There had been no rehearsal, or even instructions given, but somehow the eight men seemed to operate with a robotic precision, dipping and lifting in unison and marching in step to some silent drummer.

He had not been to many funerals and he had never been a pallbearer. As he walked down the steps to the hearse he thought of how many times he had watched the scene play out on movies and television shows and wondered whether he looked the part of the dutiful best friend: somber in his black suit at the front corner of the casket that held his most trusted confidante.

The sun was shining, and Charles thought inside himself how it's usually raining at the funerals on TV.

He rode to the cemetery with Tyler and when they arrived Trish was waiting for them. They stood at the edge of the grave, just behind Stephanie and Devin's parents. He could see Jessica standing across the casket from him and for the one second that he allowed himself to look at her she returned, and held, his gaze.

Charles quickly dropped his head and stared at the casket. He was close enough to see the pattern in the wood and he traced the lines along the lid until they disappeared beneath the bouquet of white flowers placed on top. The pastor finished his prayer, a piper began to play and

Charles watched as the patterns blurred and then disappeared. The flowers shrank and a dark shadow passed over the casket as it dropped, slowly, into the grave.

He placed a hand on Stephanie's shoulder. As she reached up and pressed her fingers around his, he could feel her shaking.

CHAPTER THREE

On Tuesdays, Charles and Tyler met during their lunch breaks to hit a bucket of balls. It was a tradition born while Devin was still alive and the result of a movie they had watched together in which two gangsters discussed their business at a driving range.

Tyler had golfed all his life. His childhood home was adorned with charming photos of a young boy in khaki pants and bright polos struggling under the weight of a bag of clubs and learning to drive a cart for the first time. For years he had pestered them, incessantly, to play a round with him and after a discussion about how the driving range was, evidently, the domain of self-obsessed businessmen who wear Rolexes or white collar criminals who drive Jaguars, Charles and Tyler relented to trying it out and found it to be a very acceptable way to spend an hour in the middle of the day. They had actually spent one very long and angry day hooking and slicing their way through 18 holes of sand and water traps before ultimately deciding that a single bucket on the range was an acceptable compromise.

In time, Tuesday's became the one day of the week when Charles made a point to wear a tie to work. The image of himself with his sleeves rolled up to the elbow, a slackened cravat dangling from his neck, swinging a 5-wood with perfect form and then shading his eyes to watch a ball sail, somehow reaffirmed and informed the man he wanted to be.

"Your swing is getting solid," Tyler said, joining Charles in admiring a particularly impressive shot. "You should really come do the front 9 with me sometime."

"Never gonna' happen," Charles said, teeing up another ball and sending it away.

Tyler accepted defeat, switched clubs and returned his attention to his tee. Charles wondered to himself why Tyler had been so drawn to golf. His footballer's frame, with bulging shoulders and weight split between two anchors, looked ridiculous swinging a thin metal stick.

"You're coming on Friday, right?" Tyler said over his shoulder.

"Yeah, I'll be there. Should I bring anything?"

"Just a starter. Trish has the rest covered."

"And by *covered* you mean she'll have made enough food for quarantine?" Charles said.

"Oh. My. God. The woman is out of her freaking mind," Tyler said, taking a swing with particular force. "She's making pasta, but yesterday brought home two hams. Just in case."

"So I should come over on Sunday too then."

"Oh yeah, just don't let Trish know or you'll have to bring fraternity pledges with you."

"That's not the worst idea," Charles said as he swung distractedly and sent a ball roughly 10 feet in front of him and 100 to the side. "They could call us 'Masters' and have to staple themselves between servings."

"I'm pretty sure you have to be *in* a frat to be pledge master," Tyler said, "Or at the very least, alumni."

"Screw that. I'm around enough juvenile assholes at work, and at least they pay me and I get to go home at the end of the day."

Charles checked his watch, slid his club back into Tyler's bag and started un-rolling his sleeves. A last-minute meeting had been called for that afternoon and he wanted to make sure he was early enough to grab a chair out of his manager's sight lines. He had about a dozen balls left and walked over to pour them out into Tyler's bucket.

"Afternoon meeting?" Tyler asked without lifting his eyes from his tee.

"Yeah, it's Sam's monthly morale-booster, where they tell us how our work is on par with curing cancer to distract us from the 10 people who were laid off this week. At least it breaks up the afternoon."

"You ever think about getting out of there?"

"And doing what, exactly?" Charles asked.

"I don't know," Tyler said. "There's got to be something you'd *like* to do."

"Not that I can think of, or at least nothing anyone would pay me for. I'd like to think I had ambition once, dreams, fantasies, but I'm an adult now – I work to live and live to work."

"Well, just think," Tyler said, making a good connection that rung out with an echoing ping as the small white ball vanished into the distance. "25 years and you can retire. Maybe."

"Hell yeah!" Charles said. "I'll be night blind, bald, and it'll hurt to piss. But I'll be free at last, free at last."

"All right man," Tyler said, setting his club on his shoulder and giving Charles a hug. "I'll see you Friday."

"Friday, yeah. Is Steph coming?"

"Yes. Well, I'm pretty sure anyway."

They both stood there, Charles pawed the ground with

his foot while Tyler shaded his eyes and looked out over the range.

"Have you talked to her at all?" Charles asked. "How is she doing?"

"I haven't. Trish said she's ok, though. They went jogging the other day."

"Good," Charles said. "Alright, I'll see you." He walked back over the lawn and gave a wave to the ball boy getting ready to head out on the range in his cage car. If it weren't for the meeting, he would've had the moving target to practice his aim on. For Charles, like most people, there was something deeply satisfying about hitting the ball car, hearing the metallic clank as the ball connected and imagining the worker jumping inside.

It made him feel, in that singular moment, like a golf sniper, like some sort of apex predator, "deadliest man on earth with a 3-wood," and – were it not for that flimsy cage – capable of ending a man's life with a single swing of his arms.

Charles wondered what it would be like to drive the thing. No matter how many times you went out and back, retrieving the balls from the range without incident while the rat-tat-tat of incoming fire bounced harmlessly away from you, the thought had to occur to you that this time, *maybe today*, the cage would fail and you would wake up in a hospital with gauze around your head, or not at all.

There had to be some part of you, he thought, that would doubt your safety despite the metal cocoon around you. It had to be a little nerve racking.

. . .

The city was hot and sticky. It wreaked of old oil and grime searing off of hot asphalt. As Charles walked along the sidewalk he was enveloped in the grimy haze of a thousand exhaust pipes and the steamy after-product of commerce. All around him was a circus of honking horns, screeching tires and the occasional obscenity, shouted at high pitch from open windows rushing past.

A blinding light was reflecting off of every glass surface and the concrete beneath his feet, attacking him from all angles. He could feel his feet heating up in his black dress shoes that caught both the sun's rays from above and the charge of friction below. Pulling his laptop bag higher onto his shoulder he quickened his pace, already feeling the tiny stings of the oppressive sun beating down on his still-winterized skin.

Rounding a corner, Charles could see the entrance to the library and the glass citadel rising up like a clean, flawless beacon. He maneuvered through the slowly-moving mass of transients, carefully twisting his body to avoid making any physical contact with their soiled and unpleasantly aromatic clothing. Most were simply muttering nonsense to themselves but a few extended their hands in a plea for the spare change that would help them buy a bus ticket home/call their daughter/score a bump of coke.

It's not that Charles was an uncharitable person. He bought at least two boxes of Girl Scout cookies each year and would often give spare change on the occasions when he had it, but typically those gestures were reserved for street performers and artists. *If you want my money*, he often said inside himself, *at least do something to earn it.*

Charles passed through the gauntlet of the living dead and reached the glass revolving doors just as the above-ground train pulled into the station a stone's throw away. In the blink of an eye the already noxious world filled with an overwhelming din comprised of sounds both human and mechanical.

With two steps, the doors swung forward, first enclosing Charles in a glass hug before depositing him safely into the calm quiet of the library interior. Inside, the air was conditioned and filled with the smells of fresh brewed coffee and potted plants. There were maybe a dozen individuals mulling about on the ground floor, taking calm, measured steps across the atrium tile, while the rest of the library's occupants sat with their eyes buried into a book, magazine or computer screen.

There was a constant noise, yes, but it was a far cry from the screeching chaos of the world outside. Here, there was but a low and steady hum made up of footsteps, chair squeaks, hushed voices and the occasional complaint of an impatient infant.

Charles felt at peace, and began making his way to his usual study table. He passed the circulation desk, pausing for a moment to look at the month's featured titles – a few young adult offerings, the latest John Grisham thriller and a "definitive special edition" of The Grapes of Wrath – before starting up the curved stair that led to the upper levels.

Once on the top floor, Charles stopped in the center of the library breezeway, the sun once again pouring in from the windows behind him. He looked out over the atrium, at the scattered people reading and sipping hot teas. Somewhere down below, tucked back inside a corner that Charles could not see, someone had begun playing acoustic guitar and singing Bob Marley's "Redemption Song.

Directly below him the revolving doors let in another guest as well as a breeze of spring air that seemed to curl up from below and spread over Charles from his toes to the top of his head. The cool air was inviting, like a gentle arm reaching up from the floor to take hold of Charles and bring him down and back outside into the sunlight.

He closed his eyes and took a deep breath. Leaning forward, he felt the weight transfer from his legs to his waist as his toes began lifting up off the ground.

"Charles?"

His eyes shot open. He was sitting at his usual table and a half-written email stared back at him from his laptop, the cursor blinking at him impatiently. Turning towards the voice, he saw Jessica standing at the table's edge looking down at him, a book in one hand and a bag slung over her shoulder.

"Jessica, hi." Charles said, fumbling as he pushed his headphones back off of his ears. He made to stand but the chord around his neck caught the slack from his laptop and caused him to land back down in his chair with a loud thump. Untethering himself, awkwardly, he rose and, more awkwardly, gave her a hug. "How are you?"

"I'm good," she replied, pulling a chair out from under the table and taking a seat next to him. "Are you doing ok? I saw you at Devin's funeral and meant to say 'Hi'."

She leaned back in her chair, her knees pressed together and pointing at him from beneath the hem of a sheer baby blue sun dress that fell dangerously high on her legs. From head to toe she was a flawless shade of light caramel, as though she had just been unearthed from some paradise that never saw winter, and Charles was suddenly possessed with a near-agonizing urge to pass his fingertips over her skin.

"Yeah, I'm fine."

The air hung heavy between them as neither spoke for a moment. Jessica was looking down at her hands, which were clasped in her lap and Charles nervously tapped a finger on his keyboard, absent-mindedly typing a long string of the letter "S".

"So, are you living in Salt Lake now?" he asked, at length.

"Yeah," she said, looking back up into his eyes. "I moved back about six months ago. Steph sent me an email about the funeral. I actually ran into her a few weeks back at the gym and we had meant to get together but could never find a good time."

Charles didn't want to talk about Stephanie, or Devin, or the funeral. "How was New York?" he asked.

"It was loud and busy," Jessica said. "The excitement wears off pretty quick. All in all it's a better place to visit than to live in. I had fun, and I like that I can say I lived in New York for a few years, but I was ready to come home. I haven't gone camping since Bush was in the white house."

Charles laughed, this was obviously a line she had used before but it brought to his mind memories of pine trees and mountain streams and Jessica in his arms as the morning sun poured in through the mesh windows of their tent. It was the end of the summer before she transferred. They had stayed up late talking by the fire and in the morning he drove her home, dropped her off with a kiss and walked away for what they both knew would be the last time.

"What are you working on?" she asked, looking at his screen.

"Nothing. Just sending emails," he said, saving the draft and clicking through to his inbox. "I canceled my wireless and just stopped to check a few things on my way home."

"You don't have the internet at your apartment?"

"No," he said with a laugh. "I had the bright idea of living more un-plugged but now I just end up spending all my time here or at Starbucks. It's good though; I live alone so it makes being home really peaceful and gives me a reason to get outside."

"Oh … you live alone," she said under her breath, almost in a whisper before adding, louder "that actually does sound nice. It seems like I only exist online sometimes."

"I know the feeling. Plus there's always good company at the public library," he said, motioning with his head to a homeless man passing their table, muttering something about Russians and basketball between a string of loud, wheezing sneeze-coughs and holding what appeared to be a dead plant in a paper cup.

Jessica glanced over and immediately swung back around, stifling a laugh and giving Charles a soft hit on the shoulder with the book she was carrying. Charles merely smiled and turned back to his laptop, scrolling through the list of new emails waiting for him. Finding nothing more to say, Jessica stood to leave.

"Well, it was so great to see you," she said, pulling the strap of her bag up and over her head.

"Yeah, you too."

She lingered there for a moment, searching for more to say before putting a hand softly down on Charles' shoulder. "See ya" she said, and turned and walked away. Charles turned back to his screen and opened up the email he was writing before her appearance. He sat there, staring at the words and letters for about a minute before shutting the laptop and leaning back in his chair, his arms crossed in front of his chest.

CHAPTER FOUR

"Oh good, you came alone," Trish said, opening the door and immediately vanishing.

"Hi, wait, what?" Charles asked.

"Nothing. Come in already, here you go," Trish said, appearing again with a small plate loaded with bite-sized hors d'oeuvres. Charles was still shutting the door behind him when Trish thrust the dish into his hands. He somehow managed to get the door closed without dropping the, now three, items that he was carrying but he gave up on moving into the room when Daniel ran up and wrapped himself around his leg. Tyler, seeing his distress, stood and relived him of the chips and dip that were dangling precariously in a bag around Charles' little finger and the bottle of wine that Charles was pinching between his elbow and side.

Less encumbered, he limped his way over to the couch and sat down to enjoy whatever delights Trish had placed in his possession. Tyler set Charles' additions down on the table and returned to his seat, groaning as he lowered himself like men of more years and girth do on television. Stephanie was sitting in a chair, balancing a plate on her knees and Trish was in a constant state of motion, organizing dishes, refilling drinks, stirring pots and making sure no one's plate ever approached emptiness.

"Trish, come sit down," Tyler said. "You're going to fill everybody up on junk before we even get a chance to eat."

"Junk?" Trish replied, aghast and mouth agape.

"Babe, just sit down."

Trish appeared annoyed but relented. Charles slid over to allow room next to Tyler but the action was arbitrary. She sat down, practically in Tyler's lap, and buried her face in his neck like a kitten.

"Hey Steph," Charles said, looking over and giving her a smile. He wanted to say more but he didn't know what. She smiled back at him and Charles decided not to force anything. Daniel apparently got bored of waiting for Charles to start walking around again and detached himself, crossing the room to pester his mother.

"Trish, this shrimp is delicious," Charles said.

"Do you want some more?" She asked, making to

stand before Tyler held her down.

"Dude, you know the rule," Tyler said. "No compliments until after dinner. We still have seven courses to get through."

"Well *excuse* me for trying to be a good hostess," Trish said, nauseatingly nuzzling Tyler's cheek with her nose.

"You're not a hostess," he said, "you're a matron."

"Speaking of which," Stephanie broke in, "how are the wedding plans going?"

Again, Trish's eyes shot open with excitement. She began opening and closing her hands, unsure of where to begin and Charles could see her eyes darting toward a bookshelf where no doubt a collection of magazine clippings was waiting. He prayed she would be unable to retrieve it.

"No, no, no, that is off limits as well." Tyler said. "Charles, say something outlandish."

"Well," Charles said, searching his mind. "I was just reading that in something like 40 percent of American households, the wife is the primary breadwinner."

"Really?" Stephanie and Trish said in unison.

"Oh come on," Tyler said with a growl. "When did we get so *boring*?"

Just then the doorbell rang. Charles looked around

the room and took a mental count, unsure of who else they were expecting. Steph seemed confused as well, but Tyler and Trish exchanged a knowing look before Trish jumped up, excitedly, to get the door. When she pulled it open, there was Jessica, holding a bowl of salad.

"Am I late?" she asked.

"No, of course not," Trish said, all but throwing her into the room. Suddenly, Trish's initial greeting dawned on Charles and he looked over at Tyler, who was looking back at him with the wide, maniacal grin that Charles liked to refer to as his "Joker face." They had set him up, Charles realized. He was trapped and the night was only getting started.

They went through another round of greetings and salutations, spending probably ten minutes making awkward small talk and munching on appetizers before a ding from the kitchen signaled that dinner – the actual dinner – was ready to be served. There was a flurry of activity as the table was set, wine was poured and dishes were given final preparations before they all sat around the table.

Charles found himself sitting all-too-conveniently next to Jessica and he wondered to himself how much planning had gone on before he had arrived. Tyler hadn't exaggerated about the food. On the table before them they had pasta with white sauce and pasta with marinara, two loaves of garlic bread, a ham, two salads, humus and pita, rolls, crackers and cheese, asparagus, Brussels sprouts and some sort of gelatinous creation with large pieces of fruit; not to mention several bottles of wine.

It was delicious and in that way that only food can it raised their spirits and within minutes the conversation was flowing freely. Tyler allowed Trish to tell a few horror stories about cake tasting and Steph broke through the elephant in the room, relating how exhausted she was of the constant barrage of well-wishers that were calling her at all hours of the day.

"The worst part is how I feel like I have to hit an appropriate balance between sounding somber and happy," she said. "The other day Devin's grandmother called and asked how I was doing. I said 'Great! I just got in from a jog around the park' and nearly gave the poor dear a heart attack. I'm fine! Devin and I had a year to get everything ready and say our goodbyes, but it's like I have to keep up appearances of gloom until everybody else is done mourning."

"Screw 'em" Tyler said. "You and Devin knew what you were doing and had five amazing years together. We all did. If people try and bring you down just tell 'em to find some other shoulder to cry on."

"Hear hear," Charles said raising his glass. "To Devin, may the lucky bastard rest in peace."

They all clinked their glasses together and took a drink. For a moment Charles caught Stephanie's gaze as she gave him a look that he couldn't quite place.

"So I hate to jump in," Trish said. "But I don't know Jessica from Eve."

"Oh," Jessica said, somewhat startled, dabbing food from the corner of her lips with a napkin. She looked like Holly Golightly, only blonde the way Truman Capote had intended, and even while eating was an image of electric beauty. "Well, there's not much to know and you probably know more about me than I do about you."

"Not really," Trish said. "You left for Columbia before I moved to the university and Charles never really wanted to talk about you that much."

"Ok, well, come on…" Charles didn't have a plan. He merely opened his month desperate to say something and simply dissolved. Everything about where this conversation was going worried Charles so he tried to jump in before it went off the rails. "Regardless of who knows who from when or where," he said. "You're really the only person at this table with stories we haven't heard before. What have you been up to for, you know, the last five years."

"Yes," Tyler said, Joker face at the ready. "Regale us with your tales of merriment and wonder. Like … are you seeing anyone?"

Charles wanted to crawl under a rock and die, but Jessica merely put on a cocksure smile and casually fired back "No, I'm not, but I don't think Trish would be into that kind of party, Tyler."

The joke cut the mounting tension in the room and after their laughter died down, without saying a word, they all seemed to stand as if on cue and make their way back toward the living room. Charles stayed behind, gathering plates and cups to carry over to the sink. Trish initially protested his efforts but Tyler made some remark about never saying 'no' to free help and took her by the arm to lead her away. Charles could see the first hints of a buzz in Tyler's face and he half-wondered if the pair would get "lost" on their way to living room for ten minutes; it had happened plenty of times before.

Jessica was still seated at the table and when Charles returned for his second load of dishes she joined him in caravanning back to the kitchen the leftover heaps of food that not in a week the group of six would've been able to consume.

They stood back to back, Charles standing over the sink rinsing off plates and silverware while Jessica dug through piles of Tupperware to give each entre a new home. She finished first, and after a moment of indecisive apprehension turned and stood next to Charles at the sink, the sides of their bodies touching and her face close to his. Close enough to smell her – some intoxicating concoction of vanilla and raspberry – and Charles could feel the muscles in his body tightening. He tried to remain as natural as possible, despite the fact that he was perpetually rinsing out a single glass that was now spotless.

It was Jessica that broke the silence, leaning in to whisper in his ear and in doing so caressing him ever so slightly with her lips.

"I miss you."

Charles shut off the water and busied himself by arranging the dishes in the sink into a more architecturally-sound pile. He refused to look at her as he spoke.

"It's been five years Jess, I gave up on missing you a long time ago," he said. His voice was callous, as hurtful a tone as his throat could muster. He could feel her body detach from his as she stepped away and his resolve faltered. "I'm sorry, it's just … first Devin, and now you're here. This whole situation is weird for me and then you have to go and say shit like that."

"Like what?" she asked.

"That you missed me."

"*Miss*," she said. "Present tense."

Finally allowing himself to look at her, he saw the devious smile on her face and felt as though he had wandered, yet again, into some sort of trap. He had no intention of wandering into another. "I'm going to get a drink, can I grab you anything?"

Charles stepped away to join the others in the living room, who were discussing the shirt Tyler was wearing. Evidently Trish had selected it for him, a pale salmon polo, in an attempt to introduce more color to the palette of Tyler's wardrobe and despite numerous protests, he had finally relented to putting it on for tonight's occasion.

"Charles, what do you think?" Tyler asked as Charles entered the room. He was pleased to have a diversion from Jessica.

"I like it," he said, "now if Trish could just do something about your hair."

Trish, thrilled to have been granted such a victory and excited by the prospect of further improvements to her man, immediately began picking at Tyler's scalp, an action that he batted away reflexively as though he was shooing a fly.

"Trish, would you don't?" Tyler said in a huff. "What do you know anyway, Charles. You like McG."

"I do not *like* McG, all I said was the last Terminator

wasn't so bad."

"The one with the girl-minator?" Jessica asked from the doorway.

"No, that one *is* terrible," Charles replied. "The one with Christian Bale."

Trish had persisted and was now straddling Tyler from behind and smoothing his hair up into a faux-hawk. "Maybe something like this," she said. "Or if you grew it out we could slick it back like Bradley Cooper. I'm sure I have a *People Magazine* around here somewhere."

Tyler merely sat hunched over with his face in his hands, a look of abject misery painted on his features.

More and more it seemed as though their conversations were dominated by the movies they had seen, the music they were listening to and the books they were reading. For years they had entertained one another with the scattered musings of a youthful mind. There was always idle talk about some melodramatic adventure, a new job or lost love, in which they could revel in and sympathize with each other's failures. But there was also passionate debates about politics and religion, questions about the duality of man and philosophical waxing on the perfect society as if they were a court of Grecian philosophers.

There's an old saying, often attributed to Eleanor Roosevelt, that great minds discuss ideas, average minds discuss events and small minds discuss people. Eleanor was a kook, but Charles had always liked the quote and remembered it every time he was asked about the last date he went on.

Now, as adults, their lives were comprised of mundane, predictable tasks. Their passions were checked, their dreams reserved and their motivations tempered. And, as if taunted by the cruel sneer of time itself, they had already been tested with the sting of a peer's death.

Life, it seemed, was full of fewer and fewer surprises.

"Well," Jessica said, "I'd better head out. Thank you so much for dinner Trish."

Trish jumped up to give her a hug, cooing profusely over how nice it was to finally meet her, how she was the prettiest thing she had ever seen and how they simply *had to* go shopping together – soon. Jessica took the adulation with a silent smile as she walked over to the door and turned the nob, before Trish stopped her.

"Oh Charles, it's dark out. Why don't you walk her to her car?"

Charles looked startled and made to stand, reflexively, before Jessica stopped him. "I'm right outside," she said. "I'll be fine, really. It was so nice seeing you all."

Trish continued to insist but Jessica merely slipped out the door and into the night. As soon as it was closed behind her, Trish spun on her heels to glare at Charles, her hands on her hips like an angry schoolmarm. "Way to go," she said. "I swear, sometimes you are just, the *dumbest* man."

A pillow thrown from somewhere near where Tyler was sitting struck Charles on the side of the face and he soon realized that everyone was staring at him. He was told, emphatically, that he had "blown it" despite assuring everyone that he had *absolutely* no idea what they were talking about.

It was getting late, and in short order Stephanie began gathering up her things and the small toys that little Daniel had strewn around the floor. Charles recognized his cue as well and followed her to the door. Tyler and Trish looked as though they were literally counting the seconds until they would have sufficient privacy to tear each other's clothes off.

Daniel protested loudly, but before the three of them were out the door he had already collapsed into a sleeping heap on Charles' shoulder. He placed the boy in his car seat, careful to not wake him, gave Stephanie a kiss on the cheek and waved them off, watching them from the sidewalk as they pulled away into the street. He turned and walked over to his car but something caught his eye as he reached into his pocket for the keys.

On his windshield, pressed to the glass by a wiper, was a small white business card. Its blank side was facing out and as he reached to retrieve it he noticed the 10 numerals, the word "Jess" and the smiling face scrawled crudely in black pen.

CHAPTER FIVE

It took Charles seven weeks to call. During that time, Jessica's card sat perched on the edge of his dresser, one-half inch away from slipping down into a wastebasket below. He saw it each day as he grabbed his socks and once again as he scooped up his keys and wallet before slipping out the door.

He told himself to throw it away. Several times he placed his hand down flat on top of the card, willing himself to slide his fingers in the most simple of gestures and be rid of the thing forever. Inside himself he wanted to cast it aside like she had done to him, as if callous indifference to an inanimate scrap of paper would vindicate the way he felt when she left.

Charles had never been much of a dater. He had spent the majority of his formative college years with Jessica and in the five years since had mostly navigated a series of flings that usually fizzled out after four to six weeks. In time, however, those became less frequent and it reached the point where Charles felt like most of the dates he went on were initiated more out of some dependence on social convention and less because he was actually interested in spending an evening with another human being.

More and more he found himself questioning the purpose of dating altogether. Unlike some men, who derived satisfaction from the mere act or the thrill of the chase, Charles found most evenings with a new acquaintance to be largely unbearable: the forced conversation, the insincerity, the rote machinations. It was like a job interview, in that you try to present the best version of yourself in the hopes of securing some imagined future that may or may not be a good fit once you get there.

As Charles got older, he realized that in most situations he simply preferred his own company to that of another person. He never had to worry about being late to a movie or finding a restaurant with vegetarian options. He could listen to whatever music he wanted as loud as he liked and he never, ever, had to impress anyone's parents. Also, there was nothing wrong with spending some time by himself. He was, after all, delightful.

But the reintroduction of Jessica into his life filled Charles with a renewed zeal for social interaction. Beginning with the day after finding her card he placed several calls to casual friends and semi-acquaintances, lining up a string of lunches and dinners like a traveling salesman in town for one week only.

He flirted with the barista, he chatted with the women on the train, he even moved from his usual spot in the library to sit across from cute twenty-somethings in yoga pants in the vain hope of striking up a conversation that could lead to meeting up for drinks.

"So what kind of books do you like?"

"I *love* Twilight."

"You *love* Twilight?"

"Yeah, I *love* it. Have you read it?"

"I have not."

"Ohmygod, it is *so* good. Did you know it was written by a Utahn?"

"Well, *technically*, it wasn't. Stephanie Meyer is Mormon and studied at BYU but she's not from Utah."

"What do you mean?"

"I mean she's not a Utahn. She's just a Mormon, and even if she was a Utahn I'm not sure why that would matter."

"Because ... we're in Utah? Whatever. It is *so* good."

After a period of this, Charles found himself calling ex-flings. He began with the most promising, the women who had always occupied the "maybe someday" and "if I had only" sections of his memory but who, for one reason of other, hadn't quite panned out.

Those dates were relatively enjoyable. They went to art galleries, listened to local music at coffee shops, tried new ethnic restaurants and walked along Main Street on rainy nights, window shopping and dipping into bistros for some dessert. They were beautiful women, in successful careers and dripping with confidence. And it took only one night for them to make it clear they were largely disinterested in Charles.

"So how's work?"

"Oh, work is great, we just bagged a big new account and (phone ringing) sorry, hold on I gotta take this. '*Hello? Oh hey Sam. No, no trouble at all, I'm just at dinner with a friend. You didn't get the report? Ok, I'll email it to you again as soon as I'm done here. The numbers look great, we're set for the presentation and those bastards are going to piss themselves. It's going to be like Christmas. No, no, I don't mean like last Christmas, I mean actual Christmas, it's going to be raining money. Yeah, yeah, I know, keep it up and I'll sue you for sexual harassment. Ok* (laughs) *shut up you old pervert, go home to your wife.*" Sorry about that. How about you, how's work?

"Oh, well, it's fine. Yeah."

"Good."

"Uh-huh."

(Takes a bite of Quinoa salad)

"So … have you seen the new Die Hard movie?"

After that round, Charles moved on to the women scorned, most of whom simply didn't answer the phone while those that did were startlingly hostile.

"What do you want Charles?"

"I thought maybe we could get some dinner? Are you free this week?"

"Is this a booty call? I haven't heard from you in six months."

"What? No, I just thought we could grab a bite."

"Look, if you think you can just call me out of the blue for a hookup you can save it for someone else Charles. I do *not* have the time."

"Claire. Calm down. Food. Would you like some?"

(Silence)

"Fine, tomorrow. Pick me up at 8."

When he finally did call Jessica, he invited her to a concert. He had already asked two other women and was about to offer the tickets to Tyler when his fingers, possessed with their own will, seized the card from its precarious nest and began punching in the digits.

She didn't question the late notice. She didn't make any quip about the 43 days it had been since they had spoken. She made no acknowledgment of the way he had received her number and how the very fact that they were speaking was a silent indication that he had given in to her ploy.

Instead, she was cordial, polite and sincere as she quickly accepted his invitation. She said she'd be thrilled to go. She knew the band, had heard they were coming to town and was excited to see them, and also Charles. He picked her up later that night. The streets were congested with traffic slowing them down as they drove in relative silence, with Jessica looking over at Charles intermittently, a wide smile across her face.

"I'm so glad you got tickets," she said at length. "I remember how much you used to talk about them but I heard their show had sold out."

"Yeah, a few weeks ago. I bought the tickets the day they went on sale."

"Is this your first time seeing them?" She had turned in her seat. Her knees were drawn up under her chin like a bird perched on a wire and the sun glittered in her eyes.

"No," he said, looking over his shoulder and focusing on completing a parallel park. "I saw them two years ago at Kilby. It was amazing, just me and fifty music friends rocking out with the band."

"Who were you going to take?"

"Huh?" he said, confused.

"You bought two tickets," she unclipped her seatbelt and shifted forward, but kept her eyes on him. "Who were you going to take?"

Charles turned to look at her. The hair around her face was illuminated from the sunlight seeping in through his window. The sun was setting, casting an auburn glow about her and the inside of the car.

"I don't know," he said, unbuckling his belt and opening the door. "Wishful thinking, I guess."

Jessica watched him through the windshield as he crossed the front of the car to her door. She accepted the hand he offered to help her out onto the sidewalk. For a moment, it seemed as though she wouldn't let him go, but he loosened his fingers to close the door and started walking inside, slightly ahead of her.

They were moving through the crowd, pushing their way toward the stage. Miraculously, the ebb and flow of pressing bodies opened a hole directly in front of them and when they came out the other side they were close enough to read the set lists. The crowd moved in tight, pinching Jessica behind him and she stood up on her tip-toes to look at the instruments on stage over Charles's shoulder.

"Here," he said, twisting his body around hers, "stand in front of me."

"They're your favorite band and I barely know them," she said, protesting.

He laughed, sliding her in front of him and leaving his hands on her hips. "Standing behind you won't block my view at all." He placed his chin down on the top of her head to emphasize his point and breathed in the intoxicating scent of her hair.

Jessica turned to say something to him but was cut off by the roar of the crowd as the band took the stage. He saw her eyes go wide with excitement just before she spun back around, putting her hands up to her face to amplify a scream.

Charles suddenly became very aware of the placement of his hands – both resting on her hips – and was about to remove them. The men on stage had barely played two chords before Charles felt her hands slide over his own, interlocking with his fingers and pulling his arms around her stomach. She rested her head back against his chest as the music swelled and to Charles it felt as though their bodies had melted together.

· · ·

A light rain had begun to fall. It wasn't enough to cause

any trouble on the roads but instead left a sheen of moisture on the windshield that sent flares of light streaking across the glass with every passing car and streetlamp overhead. They were just entering the freeway and the clouds trapped in the light of the city, filling the world with a haunting iridescent glow. Jessica was leaning back against her seat, struggling to stay awake.

"You're tired, go ahead and sleep," he said.

"No, no, that's so rude," she said, leaning forward off of the backrest and shaking her eyes open.

"No really," he said, placing a hand on her thigh. "Lean the seat back, sleep."

She looked at him as though she would protest, but the sincerity of his eyes reassured her. "Thank you for bringing me tonight," she said, laying the seat back as far as it would go and curling up into a fetal ball.

She looked angelic and after being forced to a stop by the traffic he didn't even bother taking his eyes off of her. When the cars around him began to move forward he returned his gaze to the road and, lifting his fingers from her thigh, selected a quiet playlist from his iPod to not disturb her. His attention was ahead so he didn't see it, but he felt her reach out and take hold of his hand, gently guiding it back to her leg and, turning her body to face him, pressed his and her fingers between her knees.

He thought to himself about the moment he was experiencing: a quiet drive home from seeing one of his favorite bands play, next to Jessica Warner. When she first left he had imagined a life where she would return and they would be together. After more time passed he wondered if he would ever actually see her again. Eventually, he stopped thinking about her entirely except for the sudden rush of a memory or the twisted surrealism of a dream, slipping through the cracks of consciousness as he opened his eyes in the morning.

But this? This was real. She really was in his car next to him, in corporeal form, drifting in and out of sleep and clutching his hand. He was at peace. For the first time in months his mind was free of the preoccupations of his mundane and pointless life. The numbers on his dashboard clock did not fill him with a numbing dread of returning to work Monday morning. The neon lights of a nearby grocer did not call his mind's eye back to the empty refrigerator that waited for him at home and the scrawled shopping list that had been taunting him for days from under a magnet of the Salt Lake City skyline.

Even if, one hour later when he dropped her off, he never saw her again it would be worth it for this moment, for this night. Right there, drifting along the rainy freeway at midnight, Charles felt completely safe.

PART II
FALL

CHAPTER SIX

The touch of cold metal against his stomach lifted Charles out of a deep sleep. His eyes fluttered as his pupils dilated drastically to make sense of the flood of sunlight beating against his face and slowly, dull shapes began to materialize before him and take form.

He could smell Jessica before he could see her, sitting on the edge of the bed in nothing but gray- and blue-striped underwear and a white tank top. She filled the air with her signature mix of raspberries and vanilla, the tell-tale combination of her shampoo and body wash that consequently tantalized Charles' nostrils.

"Happy six-month anniversary," she cooed, sliding a tray of food closer to his face. Her scent quickly gave way to fresh bacon, butter and maple syrup as, at last, Charle's was able to make out the details around him, including the breakfast being pushed upon him by a smiling, partially-undressed angel.

There are worse ways to be woken up, he thought to himself, propping up on one elbow and selecting the crispiest of three bacon slices.

"Six months? We're not really going to be one of *those* couples are we?"

Jessica pulled her legs up onto the bed and crossed them, Indian style, beneath her. "Oh, heavens no," she laughed. "I was just up a little early and felt like making breakfast."

"Ok, good," Charles said. He fed Jessica a slice of bacon and then sat up fully to be in a better position to eat his pancakes. "Besides, we're past six months anyway. We were dating in March."

"Noooooooooooo," Jessica said, deliberately drawing out the syllable, "the *funeral* was in March. We weren't *dating* until May because you're a little bitch baby."

"Fool me once …" Charles said under his breath, just loud enough to be heard before trailing off and placing a bite of pancakes into his mouth. He had to jerk away the fork and duck down to miss the broad side of a pillow sailing toward his face.

"Hey," he said, covering his plate, "you're going to get syrup everywhere." Jessica put on a forced pout that turned into a stifled smile and Charles reached out and pulled her closer toward him. They sat facing the door, Jessica sitting between Charles' legs with the plate resting on her lap. Charles reached around her to cut away bites and alternated between feeding himself and her.

There was a time when he would have questioned whether such scenes ever truly occurred in the living world, or at the very least scoffed at its portrayal. But as this thought reached him he quickly tossed it aside into some cluttered recess of his subconscious.

"Ok," she said, jumping up after a minute. "I've got to go."

Charles grabbed her by the wrist and pulled her back down so she was, once again, sitting on the edge of the bed. "What? I thought we were playing hooky today?"

"We *are*," Jessica said with a patronizing tone, "but I have to go home and change since *someone* doesn't like the idea of me keeping my stuff here."

"I gave you a drawer," he said, mockingly. "What more could a girl ask for?"

"Please, that drawer barely fits a pair of socks and some gym clothes. I don't even have pajamas in there."

"What would you ever need pajamas for?" Charles bit his lip in a Cheshire grin and slid his hand up the back her tank top, tickling the bumps of her spine.

"Stop it," she said, batting his hand away. "I've got to go if we're going to get out of here before noon. And don't just lie here like a bum waiting for me. If you're not ready when I get back I'm going out alone."

"Yes ma'am," he said as she stood and crossed the room. She grabbed a pair of pants off the ground and slipped them up over her legs before snatching her keys off the nightstand.

"Hey, Jess." She poked her head back into the room. "Thanks for breakfast."

Jessica smiled, mouthed 'you're welcome' and disappeared back out the door. He could hear her walking down the hall and stopping to put on her shoes. "One hour!" she called out before he heard the sound of his front door closing behind her.

Charles looked down at the plate in his hands, finished the last piece of bacon and set the dish and silverware on the nightstand before slumping back down on his back, staring up at the ceiling. He thought he would stay right there, he didn't feel like moving an inch, but as the sun rose and spread across him he felt himself begin to sweat beneath his comforter.

He slung his sheets off of him and stood, stretching his arms up with a yawn and hearing his body creak, crack and pop in ten different places. From his window he could see it was a beautiful day outside. The sun had melted the snow off the streets and sidewalks, giving everything a sleek shine like damp hair. With a glance at the clock, and Jessica's warning ringing in his ears, he slumped into the bathroom for a shower.

For about ten minutes he just stood there, letting the water roll down his naked back. He had gone from wasting time in bed to wasting time in the shower, but told himself he had plenty of it so it hardly mattered.

Jessica's passive-aggressive comment about keeping her things at his apartment was not her first and he was sure it would not be her last. So far she had avoided explicitly bringing up the subject of her moving in but it was obvious to both of them that she was slowly staking her claim on his personal space. There were no overt actions, just an accumulation of natural steps – a toothbrush here and shampoo there – that slowly turned into a full range of makeup, hair and hygiene products, organic fruits and vegetables and spare clothing items.

Charles supposed that maybe that's how it was; you spend more and more time together until one day you realize the only thing missing is her furniture and linens. It's not that he *didn't* want to live with her – he essentially did already except for the storage space a few blocks away that she visited every day – it's just that whenever he paused to think about the last six months it seemed as though he had lost all control over the progress of his life.

He wasn't sure how it was that he had arrived at this point. In his mind he recalled an image of her standing, dressed in black, on the other side of a casket and then his memory merely buzzed through a series of blurry images, the combined decisions and actions that had brought them back together, except he felt as though he hadn't had much of a say in any of them.

Charles hadn't asked her to come back. He didn't tell her to suddenly appear at Devin's funeral, then again at Tyler and Trish's dinner party. He hadn't asked for her number. He knew that he had called her and invited her to a concert and yet as he wiped the water out of his eyes he felt that same lingering feeling that it had been beyond his own control, as though he were some kind of puppet being manipulated by an unseen and omnipresent force.

But he was happy. At least he was happier than he had been before she had appeared at the funeral. *No, not the funeral,* he told himself, *it was at the library, that's where this started. She was there at the end of my table.*

Charles popped the cap on a bottle of body wash and began lathering his body, careful not to grab Jessica's raspberry garden as he had done countless times before. He laughed at the memory of arriving at work with the springy scent of fruit on his skin.

He wanted to live with her, just like he wanted to date her, be with her, and have her back in his life. But he was determined that the decision, *this decision*, would be his and his alone. She would not move in until he had asked her to do so.

As he turned off the water and reached for his towel he heard the front door open.

"You had better not be in the shower," she shouted.

"I'm getting out right now. Five minutes and I'll be ready."

He scrubbed the moisture out of his hair, hastily ran some product over his scalp and stepped out into the cold air of his room. He grabbed the first shirt and jeans he saw and a pair of socks from his dresser. He unplugged his phone from the charger and stuffed it into his front pocket and was ready to go before a look outside reminded him that it was, in fact, the dead of winter and despite the deceptive sunlight was likely freezing outside. His coat was out in the hall and he wrapped a red and black scarf around his neck for good measure before walking out into the kitchen.

"Oh, I love that scarf," Jessica said, glancing up from the morning newspaper. "You look nice."

"As do you. Ready to go?"

Jessica jumped up and pushed him across the room toward the door before he could get distracted by anything else. "Yes, let's go."

"Ok, ok, ok, hold on I have to put on my shoes."

"I'll grab the elevator," she said, disappearing around the corner. Charles dipped his feet into the pair of Alan Edmonds that he had mistreated to the point of no longer needing to untie the laces. As he was pulling the door shut behind him, he stopped, his attention caught by the impression of something foreign in the room.

It took a minute but then he saw it, placemats on his kitchen table and an upright lamp on the edge of his sofa that he recognized from Jessica's apartment.

"It's here, come on," he heard Jessica call from behind him. Charles let out a sigh, shook his head and pulled the door shut.

. . .

On Tuesday he met Stephanie for lunch. He had seen her on a number of occasions but always in a group and never with a chance to really talk since before the funeral. The weather was still sunny and clear, and despite being mid-November it was almost nice enough to eat outside on the patio. They thought about it for a moment, looking at the handful of hipster couples that were making eyes at each other over plates of caprese salad before deciding that, since Daniel was with them, they had best go indoors.

They chose a seat by the window and the sun bathed their skin, reminding them of the warmth of seasons past. Daniel lasted about two minutes in his high chair before scrambling down, around and up onto Charles' lap. It made it challenging to eat his sandwich but Charles didn't mind and Stephanie seemed to like seeing her son bond with his uncle.

"So, I'm thinking about having some sort of a get together in March," she said. "For Devin."

Charles didn't know why, but the idea seemed surprising to him. He tried to think of when Devin's birthday was and thought that it was sometime in the fall.

"It wouldn't be a celebration, and we certainly won't have one every year," she said, anticipating his thoughts. "But this first year, I don't know, I just think it would be nice to honor him somehow."

She was right, it was a good idea. There was no sense pretending that he had never lived, the proof was currently sitting on his lap playing with the green olives that Charles had discarded on his plate.

"Yeah," Charles said. "I think that will be really nice."

Stephanie described what she had in mind. A dinner party, small and quiet, essentially the core group with a few other friends and family members, maybe, well on second thought probably not. It wouldn't be solemn; maybe they could even go to a jazz club.

"Steph," Charles interrupted. "Can I ask you something?"

"Sure."

He hesitated, unsure of himself, and wiped his hands with a napkin. "Do you ever regret it?" he asked.

"What?"

"Marrying him? Having a child with him?"

Her face was pointed off to the side, looking through the window to the passers-by on the sidewalk. Slowly she turned and looked directly at him, her eyes calm and her expression fixed.

"No," she said. "Never."

"Really?"

At this she broke her gaze again. She looked down at the table where little Daniel was scribbling furiously on a piece of paper, drawing violent hashing marks over a crudely drawn face with a blue crayon.

"Do I like that my son has no father? Of course not. Do I like that I'm a 26-year-old widow? No. Does it change anything?" She was looking up at Charles again, piercing him. "Absolutely not."

Charles felt like he should drop it, but there were so many questions, so many lingering curiosities that had danced around in his brain for nearly a year.

"Do you think you'll ever get married again?"

Maybe she had expected the question, it was hard to tell. The words still struck her and she leaned back in her chair and let out a deep breath as though she had just finished some physical exertion. She crossed her ankles under the table and gazed up at the ceiling.

"I'm not opposed to it," she said. "I won't sit here and say 'I'll never love again,' but Charles, I didn't have the luxury of falling out of love with my husband like some pathetic divorcee. It would take one hell of a man to enter my life."

After a few moments, she began again. "That last night we were together? In the hospital? We both knew it was the end. He'd had plenty of scares over the years but this one was different. He was already weak and even though the doctors feigned optimism, it was clear after a few hours that he wouldn't be going home this time."

"Steph, I—"

"We didn't talk about it," she continued, either ignoring Charles or not registering him. "He pulled me up onto the bed with him and I just lay there, holding on to him for as long as I could. Daniel was in the corner asleep in a chair and just before morning Devin asked me to wake him up. I remember the way Daniel squirmed over, rubbing the sleep out of his eyes. He didn't complain. I picked him up and set him down on Devin's lap. Devin tussled his hair and said 'Danny, I love you and I'm so happy to be your daddy."

Steph's voice caught in her throat. Her eyes were wet but not teary, and she made no attempt to wipe the moisture away.

"He looked at me and grabbed my hand. He said he wanted to try and get some sleep and then he squeezed my fingers to make sure I was looking at him and he told me he loved me. I took Daniel back to the chair in the corner and sat with him as Devin dozed off."

When she finished speaking, Charles suddenly became aware that he hadn't moved in minutes. His legs were sore where the wood of the chair pressed against the back of his thighs and he shifted, uncomfortably and awkwardly and felt a rush of pinpricks as the blood passed from his waist to his toes.

Stephanie was resting her chin on her hands, with a moist glow in her eyes. The sides of her mouth were turned up in the faintest and most demure of smiles. She looked like a mother, weary with age, watching and evaluating her adult son.

"I heard that Jess moved in," she said, after a period of silence.

Charles stifled a laugh and took a sip of water. "Yup. Tomorrow, officially."

"Who's idea was that?"

"Both of ours," he said.

Stephanie waited for him to look at her, waited so that he could see the smug expression on her face. "*Sure* it was."

Charles didn't say anything. He merely acknowledged her with a self-deprecating smile and a shrug of his shoulders.

"You're unhappy," Stephanie said.

"Is that a question?"

"No. You are unhappy."

Charles opened his mouth. His tongue, teeth and lips hung there, unmoving, waiting for the signal from his brain to form words and respond.

He drew a blank.

His mouth snapped closed, producing a soft click as his teeth clamped together. Charles couldn't look at her and began shifting his eyes back and forth nervously in an attempt to evade his interrogator.

"Do you really think loving someone will make you happy?" she asked.

From beneath his brow he looked up and met her gaze, her face still angelically placed over the knuckles of her tiny hands. Charles brought his hand to his cheek and scratched the corner of his mouth.

"No," he said at length. "But I've tried everything else."

In time they finished their meal and said their goodbyes. During dinner Jessica had called and left a message that she had underestimated the time it would take to box up her things and that she would just stay at her place that night. Charles called her from the car and asked if she wanted any help but they ultimately decided she would spend one last night alone in her apartment and he could come in the morning for the heavy lifting.

After he got home, without thinking, he found himself sitting on the couch, watching old sit-coms with a giant bowl of ice cream in his lap. He made it halfway through a third episode of Seinfeld before accepting that his eyelids were spending more time closed than open. A quick glance at the ticking clock on the wall told him it was well past time to sleep.

He shuffled doggedly down the hall and collapsed face-first onto his bed. His blinds were open, painting the room with slits of orange light from the streetlamps outside. Through the walls he could hear the dull pounding of loud music. His neighbors were apparently having some sort of party, as every few minutes he would hear a chorus of laughter and at least twice the unmistakable ring of breaking glass.

He thought about calling the police. At multiple points he nearly rose up and moved back to his living room to sleep on the couch. But his resolve waned, eventually giving way to a dull, nameless desire to be disturbed by the racket. He wanted to lie there in misery, hearing nothing but the clock ticking away the hours until sunrise and the rousing chorus of laughter and revelry from everyone in the world but him.

CHAPTER SEVEN

Tyler and Trish were married on a Thursday in December. Trish had insisted on a winter wedding because of the bridal photos she had visualized in her mind. Her white dress would blend into the snowy background, with only her dark hair and dark eyes contrasting. And – this was the key part – she wanted snowflakes in her eyelashes.

To her credit, the pictures turned out to be lovely. But for Tyler it was hard to reason why their guests had to drive through a snowstorm, getting road salt on their shoes, pants and skirts just for a couple dozen shots of Trish's eyelashes. No one minded, but every time Tyler saw a member of the staff grabbing a shovel to go clear the walkway outside Charles could hear him grumbling "snowflakes" under his breath.

Charles was a groomsman. He had been passed up as

71

best man by Tyler's gangly and acne-faced teenage brother. He didn't mind in the slightest. As a groomsman his sole responsibility, as far as he could tell, was to look dapper in a tuxedo – that Trish's father paid for – and tell embarrassing stories about Tyler whenever he was called upon to do so by one of the guests. He was adequately prepared for this task, having shared in the college experience with the groom, which conveniently encapsulated a period of time in which Tyler frequently changed the style of hair on his head and other places on his body.

The bride and groom – meaning: the bride – had chosen a posh banquet hall at a resort tucked away in the mountains east of the Salt Lake Valley for their nuptials. As much as the winter irritated him, even Tyler couldn't deny the breathtaking view as the storm passed and the clouds parted, leaving a full moon and a brilliant starry sky that electrified the snow-covered dark.

The wedding "colors" were black and white, following Trish's mental image of the snowflake-and-eyelash motif. The friends had scoffed at the idea when she had first told them, but now, with the guests dancing through the hall in minimalistic, contrasting hues, the scene, both inside and out, looked like a starry winter's night.

Jessica looked stunning. She wore a sleek white dress that hugged her slender frame and yet seemed to sway like a wafting curtain. On each arm she wore a long black glove that reached her elbows and around her neck hung a string of small, irregular black stones that dipped dangerously down her neckline.

Charles watched her. Regardless of where he was, who was speaking to him or who he was dancing with, his eyes found her and he could not look away. The room seemed to flow around her, as though life were a photograph and only she was in focus. From across the hall the masses would part and sway for him to find her, guided like an orchestra by some invisible hand.

Every few songs he would tear himself away from the well-meaning aunt or precocious niece that had become his dance partner. He would pass behind her, gently taking her arm and without stopping draw her to him, their bodies twirling together with the music.

"You're stunning," he would whisper in her ear.

"It's for you," she would say, pressing the side of her face to his.

The band was a string quartet. "I want it to be like an Austen novel," Trish had said. They played a constant stream of sonatas and concertos and the guests were shocked at just how quickly they took to waltzing around the room like 18th-century aristocracy. There, blocked from view of the city below by the white-capped mountains around them, they were the bourgeoisie, the ones with stories to tell, the ones dripping with wit and charm.

But the wedding was not all pomp and circumstance. As the night wore on and the wine flowed freely, the quartet was kindly thanked for their service and relieved in lieu of an iPod attached to the in-house speaker system for Beyonce's "Put a Ring On It" – at Trish's request – and "Baby Got Back" – at Tyler's.

Little Daniel found Charles in the fray and insisted on being perched on his shoulders above the melee. After a few minutes Stephanie arrived in an attempt to "rescue" Charles, but instead the three of them danced, sometimes holding hands in a ring or with Devin high above Charles' head on his throne.

Stephanie looked relaxed and beautiful, and yet Charles couldn't help but catch a faint glimpse of melancholy sadness in her expressions. "Is everything all right?" he would shout into her ear over the music. She would answer by smiling and nodding her head but as she did the lights above would flare in the moisture around her eyes.

They danced together for probably 30 minutes.

Charles was careful not to lose his passenger as he twirled and dipped Stephanie and after a few songs she looked as though her mood had passed, laughing and smiling and snatching her son off of Charles' shoulders to twirl him about and toss him in the air.

The music stopped and after a brief lull there was a flurry of sudden activity near the kitchen. A cake was produced, a modernistic display of stacked and eschewed rectangles that alternated black and white at each level. Charles scanned the crowd for Jessica, he had lost her while dancing with Stephanie, and finally located her standing near a floor-to-ceiling window, illuminated from behind by the blinding moon. He cut through the crowd to get to her, slid his arm around her waist and stood at her side while they both watched Tyler and Trish stuff pieces of cake in each other's faces, wipe frosting from their mouths and share a messy, sugary kiss.

The bouquet was thrown, with one enthusiastic bachelorette getting a bloody nose from an ill-advised dive in the wrong direction. After that, Tyler retrieved the garter from Trish's thigh and the men lined up for their turn to squabble.

There were just less than a dozen men, of which Charles was front and center. Tyler turned his back and extended the elastic on his finger. Charles could see it coming at him, he heard the cheers swell as the lacy object sailed through the air, right at his face.

He was not a superstitious person. The garter is meaningless, he told himself. And yet, at the last moment, with the garter inches away from his grasp, his body dipped to the side and it passed him by, the lace flicking his nose as it did.

Someone behind him snatched it up. The crowd cheered. Charles applauded his victorious comrade.

The seas parted and his eyes locked with Jessica's. She gave him a coy, knowing smile, shook her head and beckoned for him to come to her with a single curved finger. He laughed and walked towards her, wrapping her up in his arms and kissing her while the crowd watched the garter and bouquet winners come together for a dance.

And then, it was over. The guests formed parallel lines and cheered as Tyler and Trish ran to their car and then, after the clatter of aluminum cans had dissipated into the night the guests, quietly resigned, gathered their things and trickled to their cars.

Jessica ran inside to get her coat and for a moment Charles was alone. A soft blanket of cloud had once again spread across the sky and a light snowfall began trickling down. He lifted his face up and, with eyes closed, felt the chill as tiny flakes touched down on his nose and cheeks.

The touch of fingers on his arms brought him back to earth and he opened his eyes to see Stephanie at his side. "We're heading out," she said, "goodnight Charles."

"Night Steph," he said, embracing her. She felt warm against his cold body and her hair smelled like coconut. When she finally pulled away from him he shivered and drew his coat closed as a rush of cold air took her place against his chest. Stooping down, he wrapped Daniel up in a bear hug and shook him, gently, side to side.

"See ya Danny Boy," he said, tossing the child's hair. "Don't let your mom get sleepy on the way home, all right?"

Stephanie opened her mouth to speak but was cut off by Jessica, who had just arrived at Charles' side. The women made their goodbyes and Stephanie, taking Daniel by the hand, walked away, giving a wave over her shoulder.

"Ready to go?" Jessica said, wrapping herself around Charles' arm and shivering as she looked up into his eyes.

It was quiet as they drove. Jessica sat in the passenger seat, dipping in and out of sleep while Charles drove slowly, contemplative. From time to time her eyes would open and he would feel her watching him, studying him.

"What's wrong?"

"Nothing, go back to sleep."

They rode the elevator up to his apartment. They

walked through the door. Jessica crossed to the closet and began shedding layers while Charles sat on the edge of the bed and loosened his tie.

"What are you thinking about?" she asked, slipping a pair of nylons off her legs.

"Devin," he said. "I mean, Tyler. He's in it now."

"What do you mean?" she walked over and sat beside him, resting her chin on his shoulder.

"I mean, he's got a wife now. After that he'll have a kid. It's some serious stuff."

"They've been together for years, is it really that big of a difference?"

"Well yeah," he said. "What if something happens to him? Before, Trish would just have an ex-boyfriend, now she'd be a …"

"A widow?"

Charles laid down on his back, his feet slung over the foot of the bed and resting on the floor. Jessica followed him, laying on her side, one hand holding up her head and the other drawing tiny circles across Charles' chest.

"I mean, how could he do that? Knowing …"

"Knowing what?"

"Knowing that he was going to die." He wasn't so much talking *to* her as he was simply talking – staring up at the ceiling with one hand behind his head.

"Tyler?" she asked.

"No, Devin."

"Oh Charles, I don't think—"

"She's a widow, Jess. Her son doesn't have a father. And it's not like it was an accident. He knew it would happen and he did it anyway. Selfish bastard."

"Charles!" she said, aghast. "Don't say that."

"No, I'm serious. How could he do that to her? How could he ask her to take that chance knowing that she would be the one to end up raising their child alone."

Jessica stood up, paced for a second and began removing her earrings. "You've talked to her about this, it was a decision they both made," she said. "I don't know why you're so upset."

"People die all the time," he continued, giving no indication that he had even heard her speak. "They choke on a piece of meat, trip down a stair case in the rain or get cancer. We all assume that we're going to live until we're 100 but we won't. A good deal of us, more than we'd like to think, will be gone one way or another by the time we're 50. Wouldn't it be better to just get it over with now? Before we leave behind a widowed wife and orphaned son?"

"Charles, stop. Why are you talking like this?"

"BECAUSE I'M IN LOVE WITH YOU!" he

shouted.

Jessica froze. She turned and looked at him but he was violently rubbing his temples with the heels of his hands, his fingers interlocked in front of his face.

"What did you say?" she asked softly.

"Anything could happen to me. I could be run over by a car tomorrow, which would actually be better because then you'd be ok. But what if I died a year from now? What if I died four years from now when *our* son is born. What then?"

Jessica walked back to the bed and crawled on top of him, peeling his hands away from his face and dragging them up over his head. She sat across his waist with her legs tucked behind her on both sides of his body.

"You love me?"

Charles rose up to lean on his elbows, bringing his face roughly even with hers. "Jess, this is serious. What if something happens to me? What if something happens to you? Devin knew his future and faced it, but we have no idea what could happen? How can we even attempt to plan for some kind of future when we have no idea what the future holds? It's terrifying. Is it really worth it?

Jessica took his face in her hands and forced him to look at her. "I want to hear you say it again."

He made a frustrated, guttural sound, and fell back

onto the bed. "You're not hearing me Jess. I'm being serious right now." Charles stared up at the ceiling. There was no sound, no movement. He could see the texture in the paint above him, he had never noticed it before. It was like the rough side of a sponge, dabbed and dotted with millions of tiny peaks and valleys. His eyes began tracing lines through the subtle pattern, back and forth from one corner of the room to another.

After a few minutes he relented and, tipping his chin down onto his chest, met her gaze. She was ready and waiting, biting her bottom lip in the kind of pose that a woman would hold in a Michael Bay movie and looking down at him from her perch on his waist. She was leaning forward, her hands pressing lightly on his ribs, which made for a striking image considering her state of undress.

"I. Want. To. Hear. You. Say. It. Again." She said slowly, in a half-whisper, articulating each syllable with pinpoint precision.

Charles thought about making a run for the door. It would be easy enough to toss her 120-pound body off of him and onto the bed – gently, of course. It wasn't like she'd be able to chase after him in her underwear and by the time she got a top and pants on he would be in his car en route to the freeway.

I wonder what the weather is like in St. George right now, he thought to himself. *I'd probably be fine without a jacket and if not, I could just keep going until I hit Las Vegas. I've always wanted to see Cirque.*

He sat up fully, pulling her in closer as she repositioned herself for the angle. As he did she lifted her hands from his sides and placed them seductively around his shoulders, she even flung her hair back with a toss of her head. *You belong on a calendar,* he thought, *not here with me.*

Charles looked up into her eyes from under his brow, a deprecated and defeated expression on his face. Jessica was beaming, patiently waiting for the inevitable and toying with him like cat. He was fairly certain she hadn't been listening to a word he said.

"I love you," he said softly. "I am *in* love with you."

She pushed him down, hard, so he laid flat on his back. Before he could form the thought of how many times he had just sat up and back down again, she lowered herself on top of him, her body stretched out over his. Their lips met. He could feel her fingers running down his chest, loosening the buttons of his tuxedo vest as she moved to whisper into his ear.

"I love you too," she said, before taking a soft pinch at his ear lobe with her teeth.

She pulled open his shirt, creating a window of flesh that stopped at his shoulders, and with one hand pulled his arm up and around her back so his fingers fell on the clasp of her bra. With that, she reached out to the wall and found the light switch and with a flick of her wrist, plunged the room into darkness.

. . .

Charles stared up at the ceiling of his bedroom, the light from a bright moon piercing through his blinds and casting long, parallel and oppressive shadows across his bed. Jessica was lying face down, her arm outstretched and draped over Charles' chest. The band of his flesh beneath it was hot and sticky from the touch.

"Jessica," he whispered, "are you awake?"

He felt her squirm slightly and heard a muffled "no" escape from where the pillow engulfed her face.

"You know what I wish sometimes?" he asked, either unaware of or unconcerned with her response. "I wish that I'd get sick. Like real sick. Like inoperable sick. I wouldn't accept treatment, wouldn't draw it out. My family would argue with me but I would hold firm. I would just let the sickness spread through my body, run its natural course and take me in due time. I'd quit my job, finish out the term of my lease and then just throw everything away and spend whatever time I had left moving from place to place with only the clothes on my back. I wouldn't leave a single dime behind. I'd finally go to Europe, to Rome and Paris and Lisbon and Venice. I'd eat great food, see amazing things, and do whatever the hell I felt like doing that day. It would be like I was celebrity, free to indulge and relax only without having to worry about being recognized or harassed by anyone."

Jessica curled up onto her side, muttered something that sounded like "go to sleep" from behind closed eyes and drifted back into the haze from whence she came. The blanket was around her waist and her bare breasts stared at him accusatorily. He thought to himself how if this was a movie, the blanket would be carefully placed to show her side, a tease of stomach and a hint of cleavage but would stop just short of exposing her nipples in the name of preserving a family-friendly and more lucrative rating.

"Eventually I'd get weaker," he continued. "I'd find some hotel with balcony rooms that I could rent week-by-week and after I lost the strength to move about whatever city I'd be in, I would simply spend the nights out overlooking the streets below, absorbing the sounds and smells. Maybe I'd write something. I'd leave a notebook dangling from my fingertips or, better yet, I'd send it to you through the post before my time came to make sure my prose didn't fall into the wrong hands."

He looked at her again. Her skin glowed a bluish-white with the light of the moon and she looked like something out of a dream.

"I'd feel it coming. I would stagger over to my bed and lay down, crippled by pain but also calm and ready for the inevitable. I would lay down on my back, just like this, and I'd turn my head to look out of the balcony doors. It would be a clear night, a bright moonlit night, and slowly the light would grow until my vision was completely bathed in white."

CHAPTER EIGHT

Stephanie circled the table, placing fork, spoon and knife in perfectly-arranged succession. She folded napkins, lit candles, arranged the chairs and asked herself for the 12th time if the red tablecloth would be better. This was a practice she enjoyed. These were elements, details, that she could control: five settings for five guests and a space for Daniel at her side.

She glanced up at the clock, the potatoes needed to start cooling and if anyone was arriving punctually she had about 15 minutes to finish her makeup and get some clothes on her child, and herself for that matter. Luckily, she thought, Trish has Tyler to slow her down and Charles has Jessica, so there was probably more time after all.

It was the first time the group had gotten together since the wedding. Between the honeymoon, the piles of thank you cards to write, the lingering wedding bills to pay and the endless amounts of newlywed sex, Tyler and Trish had barely been heard from in a month. Charles had stopped by twice, she remembered, to borrow some old tool of Devin's but had barely time to say hello with Jessica out waiting in the car.

There was something off between the two of them, she thought to herself. It wasn't anything she could name, but there had been something in Charles' eyes that day. It was a look she had seen before, frequently as a matter of fact, but had seemed to go away or at least dissipate after he and Jessica took up again. Now, it appeared to be back, which Stephanie told herself probably had less to do with Jessica than it did Charles.

It had also turned bitterly cold. Two straight weeks of cloudless winter nights had laid the earth bare to the elements. The city streets were empty, with few daring to brave the exposure and between the cold and the long, hazy dark, every action and movement seemed to slow down. It was as though the city had become a hive of reptiles, searching for warmth as their bones and muscles creaked.

After sliding the potatoes onto the range to cool, Stephanie bolted upstairs, tearing off Devin's old college sweater as she skipped up the steps. She spent a few minutes rummaging in her closet, calling out every now and then for Daniel to come into her room so she could take a look at him.

As he sauntered in, rubbing sleep from his eyes, she settled on a pair of skinny jeans that she hadn't dared attempt to fit into in months and a plain black t-shirt. After a moment's struggle with the zipper from which she gleefully emerged victorious, she caught sight of herself in the mirror and paused, running a finger across the marks on her stomach that remained from her pregnancy. They were not particularly darkened, in fact they were not visible to anyone at all beside *her*. But see them she did.

She took a step back, allowing her full figure to come into the mirror's frame. Her jeans were unbuttoned, revealing the slightest hint of baby blue underwear and from the waist upward she stood in only a white brassiere.

Like everyone, her daily routine contained a small period of nudity. But it occurred to her now, looking at her reflection, just how long it had been since she had really seen her own body. It had been longer still, she smirked, since anyone *else* had seen it.

Standing there, her arms at her sides, she could see the subtle lines of her shoulders' muscle tone, the fragile traces of her stomach running up from the waist of her clothing to her ribs. She could see the faint shading as the light from her desk lamp danced around the curve of her neck and breasts.

"Mommy," a soft voice behind her said. "Why aren't you getting dressed?"

The question was like the pebble thrown into smooth water. It startled her as she became fully aware that her child was in the room and suddenly she felt, though she wasn't sure why, mortified with embarrassment.

"Come on," she said, throwing a shirt over her head. "Let's get you cleaned up."

Charles was the first to arrive, more punctually than Stephanie would have liked. She had barely begun her attempts at smoothing down Daniel's unencumbered hair when the doorbell rang, which sent the boy hurtling out to get the door.

She called after him but it was useless and before she reached the hallway she heard Charles' voice and the sound of steps that brought him into her home. She took one last glance in the mirror in the hallway, tucking a few strands of hair behind her ear, before arriving at the top of the stairs.

"Oh," she said, looking down and seeing her son wrapped around Charles' neck. "Where's Jess?"

"She isn't here?" He asked, spinning around as though she would be hiding unseen in some corner. "I had to work late so I suggested we meet up to save time. Is no one here yet?"

"It's 7:10 Charles," she crossed the room and pulled Daniel away, setting him on the ground. "You've been around people long enough to know how this works. Do you want to call her and let her know you're here?"

"Why bother? She'll get here when she gets here."

Stephanie shook her head side to side and took Charles' coat. "Come inside, I'll grab you a drink."

Charles followed her, walking slowly and glancing at the photographs on the wall while she disappeared around a corner to hang his coat in a closet. He saw smiling portraits of Stephanie and Devin on their wedding day, candid shots of Devin holding his infant son and various memories scattered through their family's brief time together. Charles had never noticed before, but there weren't any photographs from after Devin died. Makes sense, he thought, once you've got pictures on the wall there's no point in changing them.

He entered the kitchen and pulled out a stool from beneath the bar counter. Stephanie had already arrived from the coat closet and was in the process of pouring a dark red wine into two glasses. She handed one to Charles and stayed standing, bending to rest her arms and elbows on the countertop and bringing her face down to his level.

"To my husband," she said, raising her glass.

"To my best friend." The soft clink of the glasses cut through the otherwise silent room, prompting Stephanie to dock her phone and set some music playing quietly. Within seconds the soft sound of acoustic guitar was pouring out around them, a sort of soulful rhythm you might expect to hear on a South American beach on a breezy summer evening, if such scenes actually existed in the real world.

Charles took another sip. "This is good wine," he said. "What is it."

"No idea," Stephanie said, reading the bottle. "I just asked the liquor store guy to get me something he liked. I think he wrote his number on the label."

"Yowza!" Charles said, playfully, with an over-exaggerated wink and a tip of an imaginary hat. "You still got it, baby."

"Don't I know it," she said, reaching across to top off his glass.

From his seat on the stool, Charles could see out of a small window above the sink. The sky had begun to darken under a spreading blanket of cloud and every so often a few flakes of snow would drift down into the light emanating from Stephanie's home.

Stephanie watched him as he sat, seemingly hypnotized and staring off over her shoulder. His face was lit from two competing sources, the harsh yellow from the electric bulbs above the bar on one side clashing on the ridge of his nose with the soft white of the night sky that seeped in from the window and rested on his cheek. She wondered what he was thinking, or if he was thinking anything at all, then quickly glanced over into the den to make sure Daniel was behaving himself.

The child was flipping through the pages of a large picture book, pressing his fingertips down on each of the smiling images he found, but as she watched him he cast it aside and began playing with a set of toy cars that had been left scattered on the floor.

The loud chime of the doorbell made them both jump a bit, which they reacted to with knowing and awkward laughs. Charles sat up straight and took a long draught of wine while Stephanie walked over to the door to let Jessica in.

"I'm so sorry I'm late," she said from behind rosy cheeks.

"It's nothing, Tyler and Trish aren't even … oh, here they are behind you."

The group piled into the cluttered landing and somehow wiggled the door shut behind them while removing layer after layer of coats, scarves, gloves and hats. Stephanie took the bounty in her arms and invited everyone in, where they met Charles and exchanged pleasantries.

"Sorry babe," Jessica said, kissing him on the cheek. "The damned rolls just wouldn't rise and then I had to scrape off the car."

"Really? It's *that* cold outside? It's practically March for shit's sake."

They all placed their wares on the table and gathered around Charles, where Stephanie met them and began pouring drinks. They spent about ten minutes there, chatting over each other like a roost of chickens before Stephanie suggested they'd be more comfortable around the table and, on second thought, the food is ready so why not just eat.

She had prepared some sort of chicken stuffed with heaven and covered in a melted dream and in no time at all the group had fallen relatively silent except for the staccato clink of silverware and the occasional request to pass a dish as they ravenously devoured their plunder.

"A toast," Tyler said from a partly-full mouth. "To Stephanie, for preparing this delicious meal and putting up with the lot of us."

"Hear, hear!"

"No, wait" she said, her glass still raised. "Thank you so much for coming tonight." She looked around the table at her friends, her family, and her young son at her side. "It's been one year since Devin passed away and … and I don't know how I would've made it without all of you. You've all been so amazing, to me, to Daniel. Thank you."

"To Devin," Charles said, holding out his glass and locking eyes with Stephanie.

"To Devin!" Tyler cheered. Five glasses clinked together and were drawn to ten lips. "Now," Tyler said, "to more Wine!"

"Hear, hear!"

. . .

"That's the dumbest thing I've ever heard," Tyler said. He was laying back, sunken into Stephanie's couch with one hand resting on a bulging stomach and the other lifted and tucked behind his head.

"No it's not, it's awesome." Charles said from across the room.

"You don't even listen to opera music."

"Not *yet*, but I will once I buy a record player."

"He's serious," Jessica said. She was sitting on the ground, half kneeling with her feet tucked behind her, leaning against Charles' legs with one arm resting on his thighs. "He talks about it all the time. Last week we stopped by a record store and Charles spent the better part of an hour discussing makes and models with the pot-head at the cash register.

"That guy was a genius; don't put him in a box like that."

"Anyway," she continued. "Once we got home he spent the rest of the night Googling record players and hunting through Craig's List for deals."

"Anything good?" Stephanie asked.

"No," Charles said, his voice filled with defeat. "There were a couple pieces of crap people were giving away for a song but ... I don't know, they weren't quite right."

"So, let me get this straight," Tyler began again. "You've become obsessed with buying an antiquated device you don't need, for essentially the sole purpose of listening to a musical genre you don't like?"

"It's not that I don't *like* opera. I've been to the opera. I enjoy it. It just seems weird to listen to, shit I don't know, *Vivaldi* on a freaking iPod."

"Vivaldi isn't opera, it's classical," Trish chimed in.

"Oh whatever," Charles said, waving his hand. "I want to wake up in the morning, put on some sick vinyl, draw back the blinds to bathe myself in sunlight and then conduct an imaginary orchestra in a pair of boxers and my Hugh Hefner bathrobe like some European Bad-Ass. I want to be more cultured and impressive, like Daniel Day-

Lewis in My Left Foot."

"Only, with the use of your hands," Trish said.

"Fine then, like Colm Feore in Sum of All Fears," Charles offered.

"Except ... without getting your throat slit by Liev Schreiber?" Trish asked, timidly.

"Remember when he was in 24?" Tyler asked. "How awkward is the title '*First Gentleman*?'"

"I like the name Liev," Trisha said. "What if we named our –"

"Absolutely not," Tyler cut in, nipping the idea in its bud.

"I feel we're getting off topic," Stephanie said, hiding her face in her hands so Charles would not see the smile she was suppressing. Even so, he glared at her, then the remainder of the group, with fixed eyes like a sulking, naughty child.

"Oh, lighten up," Jessica said, hitting Charles lightly. "We're just giving you a hard time. It sounds wonderful and I can't wait to see you leading the overture in your underwear."

"That's good, since he'll expect you to give him a standing-*Ohhhhhh*," Tyler said with wide eyes and a coy smirk, slowly raising his hand in the air in waiting.

A shadow passed over Charles' face. It occurred to

him, in that instant, that this fantasy had never included a third party. In his mind's eye it was always just him and the music, filling the space of a small, brightly-lit apartment on some carefree weekend morning with the smell of fresh coffee and cooking bacon wafting in from the kitchen.

The rest of the group was laughing at Tyler's inappropriate, albeit derivative, joke and within seconds the sound was replaced with an awkward silence as they all became aware of Charles' daze.

"Come on man," Tyler said, his hand still outstretched. "Don't leave me hangin'."

Charles awoke and leaned forward to return the high-five. "All right," he said, making contact. "You earned it, I suppose"

"Speaking of which," Trish said, her eyes lighting up. "Now that you guys are living together, how long until … well?"

"Seriously, Trish?" Tyler said, grabbing his wife in a playful, but effective, headlock.

Charles looked stricken with abject terror and Jessica, noticing this, attempted to diffuse the situation.

"I don't know," she said, turning to look up at Charles. "Maybe sometime in the fall?"

"Wait, what?" His eyes rapidly shot back and forth from the several faces that surrounded him, occasionally landing on inanimate objects around the room as though a lamp or mantelpiece could save him from this nightmare. In the flash of a second he felt a wave of heat fill him as perspiration formed on his brow and the beat of his heart quickened. He looked as though he had just stepped off some carnival ride and was having trouble focusing as the world continued to spin around him.

"Woah, woah, woah. We have never talked about '*the Fall*'. We've never talked about this. What the hell are we even talking about?"

"Babe, relax. I'm not saying you're out buying a ring or anything. I just figured, it's been almost a year now, plus the time we dated in college."

"Now hold on, that does NOT count!" Charles said, his voice suddenly taking on a forceful edge.

"Of course it does," Trish said, adding to the already noticeable level of discomfort on Tyler's face. "Everything counts."

"No!" Charles said, turning away from the woman at his feet to appeal to the group. "She left me. She abandoned me in the blink of an eye like I was nothing. One night I was sitting by a campfire with my girlfriend and the next morning she was gone. Poof! On a plane to New *fucking* York."

"Charles," Jessica said. She had turned toward him

now, both her hands resting on his legs and staring up into his eyes like a purring kitten. "I'm sorry, I didn't mean anything by it. We don't have to talk about this."

"You know what she said to me?" He said, ignoring her. "That night? She said that I would be a distraction, that if I was in her life then she might throw in the towel on her *career* after any old bad day and come back to Utah." His lips lingered on the word 'career' as though it was some kind of vile, disgusting thing.

"She said that for her to be successful she needed to cut ties and assume that she was never coming back. Because ending up in Utah would mean she had failed. Being here, with me, would be a consolation prize compared to living her big dreams in the big city with her big success."

Then he turned to her. He looked at her, but he did not speak to her. Instead he spoke *through* her, in the way people speak to their reflection in a mirror or make a wish before casting a quarter into a well. Only his words were not encouraging or hopeful, they were filled with years of bitterness and pain.

"And now ... here we are."

Stephanie cautiously reached out, her fingers slowly cutting through the air before coming to rest gently on his shoulder. "Charles –"

"Mommy," Daniel had appeared at the mouth of the hallway, one hand dangling a stuffed toy while the other rubbed sleep out of his eye. "I'm tired."

"Oh darling," Stephanie said, reaching out for the boy. "Have we been keeping you up? I'm so sorry baby."

"Come on gang," Tyler said, lifting himself out of the couch with considerable effort. "That's our cue."

The group began to slowly remove themselves from their seats and gather their things. Charles made to stand but Jessica's weight was still on his legs, holding him down. He looked down at her, seeing her, truly, for the first time in minutes. She made no attempt to hide the pain in her eyes and as he looked at her she reached up and put her hand on the side of his head, her thumb resting off of his cheek.

"Charles, I'm so sorry," she said. "For everything. I'm sorry I brought it up and we don't ever have to talk about it if you don't want to."

She was beautiful, almost more so with her big wet eyes staring up at him like some anime cartoon character. He could feel his pulse pounding in his forehead, a combination of both his tirade and the alcohol pulsing through his veins. He could feel his resolution slipping, the words "I'm sorry" were forming on his lips when he felt a tug on his sleeve.

"Tuck me in Uncle Charles," Daniel said, appearing suddenly at his side.

Stephanie arrived just as quickly to scoop him up. "Charles has to go home now Daniel, say goodnight."

"No, I'll take him," Charles said, standing up and extending his arms. "I'll tuck him in while you see everybody out."

Stephanie looked at him incredulously, her eyes bouncing between him and Jessica who had lifted herself up off the ground and was now standing behind Charles' shoulder. "Are you sure?" Stephanie asked, with a voice that suggested his time might better be spent in other pursuits.

"Yeah, give him here," he said, taking Daniel from her. The child laid his head down on Charles' shoulder as he turned back to face Jessica.

"It's ok," Charles said, reaching out with his free hand and gently stroking her arm. "It's ok. I'll see you back home in a few minutes."

"Ok," she said, wiping a hand down the corner of her eye. She straightened herself up, and with a firm blink opened her eyes with a fixed smile on her face. It was all it took for her to transform back into the poised, confident woman she always was. "Stephanie, thank you so much for having us tonight. Dinner was lovely."

"Oh, thanks for coming Jess," she said, accepting a hug before leading Jessica to the door where Tyler was helping Trish with her coat. Charles passed to the staircase and gestured silently to the sleeping Daniel, throwing a smile and a wave at his friends. Before he turned the corner he caught one last glimpse of Jessica, standing in the doorway as the now-heavy snow fell just behind in her, illuminated by the porch light against the backdrop of a dark, black night.

The carpet helped him walk stealthily to Daniel's nursery where he laid the boy down and smoothed the blankets around him, pinning him inside like a small, precious gift. He stayed there for a moment, kneeling beside the tiny bed and listening to the steady breaths. For the most part Daniel had taken after his mother, but in the low light, blissfully asleep, Charles could see Devin's face in the child's soft features.

As he stood, he caught sight of an envelope on the window sill. It was cream-colored and frayed along the edge from where a finger had passed under the fold and broken the adhesive seal. On its face, in crude lettering that looked like it was hand-drawn in crayon, was scrawled the word "Daniel" and the number 4.

Charles plucked it up. Inside was a piece of heavy cardstock folded once. He slipped it out of the envelope and opened it up, quickly recognizing the handwriting.

Daniel,

Happy fourth birthday! I'm sorry I couldn't be there with you and mommy, but I wanted to tell you how much I love you and how happy I am to be your dad.

I want you to be extra nice to mommy. She's the best mom in the whole world so be good and do what she asks you to.

I hope you're enjoying preschool and have the best birthday ever. Tell mommy that I said to let you pick any flavor of ice cream you want.

I miss you and I love you,
Dad

Stephanie placed a hand on Charles shoulder. He had not heard her enter the room but it did not startle him. They walked out of the room together, flicking the lights off as they passed and carefully shutting the door behind them with only the slightest creak of its hinges.

They found themselves face to face in the narrow hallway, the only light coming from far away on the lower level.

"What was all of that?" she asked in a whisper.

"What do you mean?"

"You know what I mean," she said, placing a hand on

his arm. "Are you ok?"

"I'm fine," he said. "I'm fine. I don't know what I freaked out about. I'm just in one of those moods."

"And how long have you been in '*one of those moods*'?" she said.

Charles broke her gaze and looked down at his feet, which he then shuffled back and forth like a schoolboy waiting for his punishment. "Does it feel like it's been a year to you?" he said. "It's just, what you said tonight and the way I've been feeling lately. I feel like the days just go by and then when I stop to catch a breath I remember that I'm with Jessica now and that it's been so many years and yet all I can remember is her leaving. I play it over and over again in my mind, trying to remember what I felt then and asking myself how I should feel now."

"I mean," he continued, "you were there. You remember how I was after. Don't you think five-years-ago Charles would kick my ass for taking her back like this?"

"I don't know Charles," she said. "What happened, happened. You shouldn't forget it but you can't let it hold you back either."

He stopped speaking. He stopped shuffling his feet and for a moment, he stopped breathing. Then he lifted his head and looked at her.

"I just miss him so much, Steph," he said. "I don't

really know why but I just miss him so much. It should have been me. You've got Daniel and oh God, it should've been me."

Tears were now flowing freely down his face as his hunched shoulders shook between lurching sobs. She wrapped her arms around his neck and pressed her cheek to his, her fingers knotting and un-knotting the hair on the back of his head. He pulled her tight against him at the waist and could feel her shoulder twitch against his collarbone as she too fought back the urge to cry. He could feel her quick, staggered breathing in his ear and a trembling in the fingers that had fallen to beneath his shirt collar.

Then he felt her lips, cold and quivering as they slipped between his, the sharp intake of breath as he squeezed her tighter and the warmth of her body pressed against him as he pushed her against the wall. He felt her tongue darting in and out of his mouth and running along the ridges of his teeth. He felt her weight shift to his arms as her legs began to give out beneath her and a chill ran through his spine as she clawed at his chest and stomach.

Abruptly, almost violently, he released her and stepped away, his features a mask of shock and confused horror. He stumbled clumsily down the hallway and stairs, throwing himself out her door and into the cold street. If she had called out or attempted to stop him he did not know as he was blind to all sight and sound around him.

Charles didn't feel the keys turn in his hand or hear the engine roar to life. His sight somehow kept the car in motion as his brain attempted to make sense of the cluttered and inconceivable information it was receiving. He could smell her and taste her, sensory puzzle pieces that accompanied little flashes of memory that he could not process.

He did not see the snow falling outside, the way the beams from his headlights drifted away from the center line or the occasional tremor in his steering wheel as the wheels lost traction on the wet pavement. When the sharp curve approached, the car did not turn.

He did not feel the shift in weight as he left the ground or later the pain as he was rocked side to side, forward and back.

He did not hear the roar of the engine as his wheels spun freely in the air, the loud crack of the car's frame plunging into the snow or the thunder of shattered glass and twisted metal.

And after a few moments, he did not see, feel or hear anything at all.

CHAPTER NINE

Dust flew up from under the wheels of Charles' car as it barreled down the desolate country road. Inside, Jessica sat in the passenger seat, staring out her window with a look of discomfort as the Toyota bobbed up and down and shook violently in its frame.

Her long hair was pulled back into a loose ponytail, with stray strands falling against cheeks that shone as the setting sun poured in from the window. Charles' did not notice any of these details. He was busy shouting into his cellphone, which at this exact moment was pressed between his shoulder and jaw as he tried with both hands to steer the car clear of boulders and other debris scattered across his path.

"I'm telling you," he said, tersely. "I've already gone five and a half miles and … Hey! … can you hear me?

Shit, if I lose you we're screwed. You there? Ok, I hear you. Wait ... wait, ok I think I see it. Yeah, fork in the road and I go left? LEFT? Got it."

"How close are we?" she asked passively.

Charles stole a furtive glance at her, registered the look on her face and lowered his voice to a calm hum. "He says it's about two miles from the fork. Straight shot. We're just going up that hill and across the river."

Satisfied, or at least seemingly satisfied, Jessica nestled back into her chair. She set one hand on her forehead and the other across her stomach and curled her body away from him into a sort of buckled fetal position.

"Hey, you OK?" he asked, reaching out and placing a hand on her thigh.

"Yeah, just carsick," she said, turning herself farther from him.

They had been driving for about 90 minutes and the last 30 had been particularly unpleasant. Charles grew up in the country but even he had to admit that the rocky, uneven path they were currently bouncing along was interminable. He looked back at Jessica, wondering what he could do to make her feel better but realized quickly that he wasn't precisely sure what was wrong. She had been quiet for most of the morning, beginning when he arrived at her apartment to pick her up.

Rounding a corner, a short row of familiar vehicles came into few. Charles breathed a sigh of relief and swung his car into an empty slot between Tyler's Jeep and a downed log. He could see a thin wisp of smoke snaking up into the air and followed it down to where his friends sat around a small fire. Tyler was crouched down on all fours, red-faced from blowing on the flames and tossing wadded-up bits of newspaper in between the small tepee of logs he had apparently constructed – hastily, it appeared.

Charles unbuckled his belt and reached for the handle of his door, but with a sudden movement Jessica grabbed his arm and pulled him back into his seat.

"I got in," she said, a just-perceptible tremor in her voice. "I got accepted."

"Babe, that's great," he looked at her wide-eyed and leaned in to kiss her but felt the push of a hand on his chest as Jessica resisted. "What's wrong?"

She dropped her hand and turned away from him, facing out of the front window. "We have to stop seeing each other," she said coldly.

He stared at her, unblinking, his face frozen in daft and wordless confusion. At the camp, Stephanie stood between them and the fire, watching them. As she and Charles locked eyes he could tell that she had been walking over to say hello but had stopped dead in her track about ten feet away. He dipped his head at her in some sort of visual cue, unsure of what message he intended to convey but relieved that she seemed to understand as he saw her turn slowly and retreat back to the campfire.

"Jess, what are you saying?" he asked gently. She reached a hand up and wiped her eyes.

"Charles," she said. "I have to do this, It's what I've been working toward for three years and it could change my life."

"Of course, but –"

"And I have to take it seriously, which means I can't go out there thinking that I'm going to rush home to you as soon as it's over. I can't have one foot in *Utah*. If I'm going to do this then I have to believe there's no coming back."

"Ok, I understand what you're saying, but ..."

There was no but. He did understand. It angered him. He felt a dull fog creeping around him at the thought of her leaving but he still had enough of a head about him to understand her meaning. "But do we have to decide this now? You're not going to be leaving until –"

"Wednesday," she said, cutting him off midstream.

"What?"

"Wednesday. I'm leaving Wednesday."

"Wh...bu...why?" he stammered. "The semester just

ended. They wouldn't be expecting you for three months. At least."

"I want to get out there as soon as possible. Find an apartment, settle in, and familiarize myself with the city. I want to look like I belong on the day I start."

"Jessica hold on, can't we just …" she didn't interrupt him, he merely trailed off. The rest of the group could tell by now that something was wrong. Charles could see several pairs of eyes stealing fleeting glances in their direction, despite their best efforts to hide the fact that they were staring.

"I'm leaving on Wednesday," she said after a period of silence. "I'm moving to New York and as far as we're concerned I'm never coming back. I'm sorry. God, I'm so sorry Charles but this is the way it has to be. I found out a few days ago and I wanted to tell you but I had to make up my mind before you were able to talk me out of it. There's no point now, I'm not going to change my mind."

"No," he said. His voice sounded hollow, distant. "I won't try."

Charles took hold of the handle and opened his door. He made calm, deliberate steps around the car and retrieved his bag, tent and camp chairs from the trunk before walking toward the rest of the group. Jessica, in her own time, made her way out of the car and followed him.

Everyone exchanged their 'hellos' before Stephanie made some excuse – a salad to prepare, drinks to mix, et cetera – to pull Jessica away. Charles sat down in a folding chair facing the fire and began poking at the glowing logs with a stick. He didn't bother looking over his shoulder as she and Stephanie slipped away, arm in arm, toward the picnic table, whispering in hushed, hurried tones. He had not, in fact, looked her in the eye since exiting his car.

"What's wrong, man?" a calm voice asked on Charles' left side.

Charles didn't turn, he could see out of the corner of his eyes a pair of hands carving small intricate designs into a long, thin branch. They were large hands, but without callous. The long fingers worked the knife and wood with precision dexterity and despite frequent quick, jerking movements appeared to flow evenly as though they were directing a tiny symphony.

"Jessica just dumped me," Charles said.

Tyler looked up from his post as blower of the flames, frozen with his mouth gaping open mid-gust. "Come again?" he asked, bewildered.

Devin stopped his whittling and, without a word, reached into a cooler at his feet and handed Charles a drink. "You want to talk about it?"

"Nope!" Charles said loudly before popping his bottle

cap into the fire and taking a long swig. After draining half the bottle he dropped his head and wiped his mouth with a sleeve. "She got into Columbia, which apparently means she's leaving for New York this week."

"So," Devin said. "Did you want to talk about it then?"

"No," he said, stifling a laugh. "Bastard."

Contended to oblige his friend's wishes, Devin dropped his head and resumed his masterpiece while Tyler continued to stare in wide-eyed protest for several minutes. Eventually, he accepted that he would receive no further details and went back to his work of building the fire.

"Not to be insensitive," Devin said quietly, after a long period of silence, "but me and Steph are getting married," Devin said quietly.

"Ok, seriously?" Tyler said, falling back into a seated position on the ground. "What?"

Charles was stunned. He immediately whipped his head around to look back to where Stephanie and Jessica were standing, as if for some reason she was in danger of disappearing because of what he had just heard. With equally quick action he swung his head back around to face Devin.

"Dude is that …," he sputtered, before dropping his

voice to a lower volume. "Is that really such a good idea? Right now?"

"Yeah man, it is."

"But," he said, his voice lingering.

"It's ok," Devin said, "you can say it."

"But what about your cancer?" Charles leaned forward and whispered, as though he was uttering a dirty, forbidden word. "Don't you think you should give your remission more time?"

"To what end?" Devin said, setting on him with a firm look. "We're going to get married. That's final. If my cancer returns, hell, if I die, then the last thing I want to do right now is postpone any more of my life."

"But what about Stephanie?"

"This wasn't *my* decision," he said. "When she first brought it up I had the same reaction as you. Believe me, the last thing I want is to make her some sort of early-30's widow. But you know what? Most women probably wouldn't have even given me the time of day with all of my baggage but not Steph. She's the best thing that ever happened to me and if she wants to marry a guy with leukemia who the hell am I to say no? Besides, she's the one that is going to have to deal with that scenario, not me."

"Dude!" Charles said, reproachfully.

"You know what I mean," Devin said, a coy smile on his face.

"Well man," said Tyler, who had satisfied himself with the size of the fire and was now sitting down flat in the dirt. "Congratulations?"

"Thank you Tyler," Devin said, taking a sip of his beer. "Oh yeah, we're going to try to have a baby too."

"Oh God," Charles let out a deep groan. "Wait, can you even? With the chemo?"

"They put some of my stuff on ice when I started," Devin said. "The Doctor says there's still a good chance we can do it naturally, but if not there's always the alternative."

"But Dev, come on," Charles said with a hint of pleading in his voice. "If you have a baby and then … you know."

"Yeah, I know. It sucks. The whole thing goddamn sucks man, but I guess if something happens to me then at least there will be someone there to look after her."

"Dude, you know we'd look after Steph," Charles said.

"I know, I know," Devin said. "But I mean family. In a way it's nice to know that if something happens then it won't have all been for nothing, you know? Besides, as long as I'm breathing I gotta live my life. I can't just live in fear."

"Fear of widowing your wife and orphaning your child seems like a pretty rational fear to me," Charles said. He immediately regretted it. He could see a chill pass through Devin as he clenched his jaw. A look of veiled anger mixed with a creeping sadness filled his features.

"I'm sorry man," Charles said. "That was a dick thing to say. I'm happy for you, I really am and whatever happens I'll look after your family."

"Me too," Tyler said.

"All right," Devin said, straightening up and taking a deep breath. "That's enough of that talk. Now, where all the white women at?"

. . .

The evening passed, pleasantly and without incident. Charles and Jessica maintained what could be described as an armed neutrality, neither addressing each other directly nor outright ignoring one another. They sat apart and from time to time Charles couldn't help but look over at her. Each time he did he found that she was looking back at him, with a pleasant and inviting smile on her face that only seemed to make him boil with rage.

In the planning of the Cancer-Free Celebration Camping Trip, they had talked about walking through the woods, skipping stones across streams, maybe even doing a little fishing. But as they sat around the fire, laughing and joking, roasting hot dogs and s'mores, the time effortlessly slipped away. In no time at all the sun said it's last goodbyes and a bright moon and twinkling stars took its place.

A wind rustled the trees, adding a soft percussion of leaves to the chirping chorus of crickets and the other creaks and cracks of the mysterious night. With the setting of the sun the temperature dropped rapidly and inch by inch the group slowly closed ranks around the fire.

"I'm just saying, there's more to Rand's Objectivism than just being a self-centered jerk," Charles was saying. "If everyone worried about taking care of themselves, and if we as a society encouraged production and contribution instead of mediocrity and entitlement, then we'd be better off in the aggregate."

"Charles," Stephanie said, shaking her head. "I'm not about to spend the time to read a 1,000-page manifesto on the merits of conservativism. Maybe after I graduate when I actually have time to read for pleasure, although I'm not certain the term 'pleasure' would even apply here."

"It is not a conservative manifesto, that's just a superficial generalization made by people who don't fully understand the text. It's largely a criticisms of social conventions, like how we allow people to guilt us into doing things we don't want to do and how we, collectively as a society, reward and aspire to laziness."

"Oh Gaaaaaawd, shut up about Ayn Rand already," Tyler said before stuffing a particularly large and gooey marshmallow into his gaping mouth.

"Well," Devin said with a yawn. "I don't care what any of you have to say, I'm going to bed and you can't guilt me out of it."

"Lame," said Tyler. "It's nice for the four of you, you don't have to freeze to death in a tent by yourself tonight. This fifth wheel shit gots to go."

"Why didn't you bring that girl that keeps calling you?" Stephanie said as she helped Devin to his feet. "Your ex from high school. Tessa? Tracy?"

"It's Trish," Tyler said. "And no way. That bitch is cray-cray."

"Classy," Charles said, rising to his feet. "Well, I guess I'll hit it too." It occurred to him at that moment that he wasn't sure what the sleeping arrangements were anymore. Was Jessica expecting him to crash in Tyler's tent now?

Whatever, he thought. *If anyone's going to get squished by that oaf it's her.*

"Yeah," Jess said, sensing the thought process going on his head. "I'm coming."

They walked silently away from the fire, where Tyler

was defiantly opening up another bag of marshmallows and his fifth beer. *We'll probably find him right there in the morning*, Charles thought.

Inside the tent, Charles began spreading out their sleeping bags while Jessica pulled off her smoky clothes. The night was not going at all as planned, a realization further punctuated for Charles by the sight of Jessica in her underwear.

"Jess," he said at length. "I get it, I really do. And yeah, I'm mad – I'm pissed – but I'm happy for you."

"Thanks Charles," she said, glancing at him over a bare shoulder.

Charles swapped his jeans for a pair of gym shorts and slipped down into his bag. The ground beneath him was rough and uneven and he cursed at himself for once again shorting himself on padding in the interest of "packing light," an unfortunate quality instilled in him by his economical father. He squirmed both inside and out, twisting his body to find the most comfortable position and fruitlessly willing his mind to expel the image of Jessica lying next to him in nothing but a pair of panties and a tight-fitting tank top.

"I just ..." he said, searching for the words. "Why did you have to tell me today? Couldn't you have waited till we were home? I mean, this is our last trip together. It would've been nice to enjoy it."

She moved like a cat.

In an instant, and through movements that seemed to defy physical law, she was inside his sleeping bag, her body pressed against his.

"Who says we can't enjoy it?" she asked, running her hand down his stomach and under the waist of his shorts. "I just said we had to stop seeing each other. I didn't say we had to stop tonight."

When their lips met, they did so with an added ferocity intoxicated by the knowledge of their last night together. His mind raced to catalogue every taste, sound and sensation: the warmth of her skin covered in a sheen of sweat, the rhythm of her breathing, the tips of her fingers pressing down on the back of his neck.

Charles pulled her body tightly against his own, feeling the strain in his forearms. He wanting to absorb her, consume her. It was as though she was already beginning to slip away and would be lost and gone when he opened his eyes if he relaxed his grip.

CHAPTER TEN

Charles began to emerge from the haze long before his eyes opened. He could feel consciousness spreading through his body, with the tingles and shivers of life flushing through his veins.

He felt groggy and his head hurt but he was present enough to deduce his surroundings even while his eyelids fought to stay closed. His legs were weighed down by a stiff, itchy blanket. There was a pinch and pressure in the crook of his elbow where cold metal penetrated his skin. From underneath a tightly wound bandage his head throbbed and pulsed and all around him he could hear the whir and buzz of electronics.

"*I'm in a hospital*," Charles thought to himself, "*I'm alive.*"

He felt disappointed.

Immediately, he began to think about the ramifications of his resurrection. He had clearly been knocked out by the accident, which meant he likely suffered a severe concussion, if not other, more serious injuries. His toes and fingers wiggled on command. He was stiff, but beyond his throbbing head he didn't register any shooting pains as he tested flexing the various muscles in his body. Of course, he could be loaded with any number of pain medications, so who knows how bad he might feel it in the morning.

Actually, it was probably morning already. He must have been transported by ambulance and kept overnight, which meant thousands of dollars in medical bills that in the best case would drive up his insurance premiums and in the worst case cripple him financially. He had insurance, he reminded himself, but it occurred to him that he had never really needed to use it before.

He'd read that article in TIME. That saline solution or sugar water or whatever other crap they were pumping into his arm was probably drip-dripping at $100 a bag. Charles was pretty certain his insurance had a payout limit but damn it if he knew what it was. Besides, like any American adult he had heard plenty of HMO horror stories and for all he knew his provider might give him the run-around for his near-death experience not being preapproved. *I'll call you the next time I...*

It was then that he remembered why, in all actuality, he was in the hospital.

Stephanie, he thought, *we kissed, and then I drove into the side of a mountain.*

Or ... she had kissed him. Right? He played what he could remember over in his mind and while he came to the conclusion that she had kissed him he wasn't quite sure how he had reacted or, better still, why. Had he pushed her away immediately? Had he lingered? Did he really care one way or the other? Well, he thought, you're in love with Jess and *she* might have something to say about it.

Who am I kidding, he thought, you can't just kiss Stephanie. Who cares if you have a girlfriend, she's *your best friend's wife!*

Except, Devin was gone. He didn't wake up from *his* accident. He didn't have to worry about what his girl would think. He didn't have to explain himself or face the world. He sure as hell didn't have to pay his hospital bills. Stephanie had to shoulder everything: the pain, the loss and the burden.

The weight on his eyes slowly began to lift. He could feel his lashes separating with a slight, sticky resistance. His vision was first a sliver of light that then gave way to an omnipresent haze.

He didn't wonder about how his face and body would look when his vision focused. He wasn't curious what time the clock on the bedside table would read, or even what day. Instead, he found himself recalling a thought that had played in his mind countless times during the course of his admittedly uneventful existence. Charles had often wondered to himself who, should he ever find himself waking up in a hospital, would be sitting at his bedside.

Would Jessica be curled up in some awful contortion, fighting off an uneasy sleep in a chair against the wall? Would Daniel be coloring in a book on the floor while his mother paced back and forth? Would Tyler and Trish have stopped by at just that exact, opportune moment. Had anyone even thought to tell his parents?

In his mind he imagined opening his eyes to find his friend Devin, reading the Sports Illustrated Swimsuit edition or, better yet, flirting innocuously with some bombshell orderly. Charles would stir, groaning as the pain reached him and Devin would turn over his shoulder and flash a Cheshire grin. "Hey," he would say, "look who's late to the party?"

Charles blinked, drawing fresh moisture across his eyes. It obscured what little vision had materialized but within moments the clouds pulled back like fog on a windshield. He could see clearly now, the numbers on an electric monitor, the visual diagrams by the door, television and light switch, the door to the bathroom in the corner.

His could also see, without bothering to turn his head, that he was completely alone.

. . .

The doctor told Charles that he had sustained two fractured ribs and a broken collarbone from the seatbelt, burns on his arms from the airbag and, yes, a severe concussion and several stitches from putting his head through the driver's side window. According to the authorities, had he not been wearing a seatbelt he would have most likely been ejected from the vehicle and then crushed after it rolled over him. At one point he thought he heard the phrase "near-decapitation" but it was unclear. Thanks to a strip of polyester and nylon, however, he would walk away with his arm in a sling to go home and pick pieces of glass out of his hair and face sporadically over the next several days.

He wondered how many sick days he could milk out of his injuries before he'd have to return to work. For several weeks he had been considering leaving his job to transition to something new, but obviously that was no longer an option. Charles couldn't afford to be unemployed right now, a reality that was glaringly obvious to him with every beep of hospital machinery.

Charles felt trapped. Trapped in an unfulfilling career in an unfulfilling life and, more presently, trapped in bed with a needle in his arm.

It took several hours before Jessica arrived. By then he was already sitting up in bed and had enjoyed several cups of chocolate pudding. She entered the room in a huff, throwing down her purse and coat and making apologies for coming "as soon as she could." The chair squeaked across the floor, sliding a few inches as she all but jumped into it. She reached her arms out toward his face but immediately snapped them back as if they were on invisible springs, fearful that in his damaged state the slightest touch would cause him to crumble into dust.

"Charles," she said at length, "Oh my God, Charles, are you ok?"

"They tell me I'll be fine," he said.

"We came last night when we heard but they had you sedated, something about trying to keep your head from swelling. I called your insurance so everything is taken care of there, they're just waiting to hear back from the police on the accident report."

"Oh good, so I have an interview with the police to look forward to as well."

"The doctors told me last night your blood-alcohol was under the limit," she said. "I wouldn't worry about it, there were a lot of accidents last night. The roads were terrible."

"That had nothing to do with it," he said.

She looked at him apprehensively. Neither one of them had any illusions about the cold way he was receiving her and he could see the machinations of her brain operating as she carefully chose her words and weighed everything that was happening.

"I talked to Stephanie," she said quietly, in a hushed but quavering whisper. "She told me what happened, that you … It's ok, it was a weird night with Devin and with, everything. I'm not mad."

She reached out and took his hand in hers. Her sincerity was palpable, her smile both genuine and forgiving. He saw it then, the subtle traces in her beauty that betrayed the long night of worry she had been through. There were shadows beneath her eyes and she wore only the slightest amount of makeup. Her clothes were the same as the night before and he wondered if she had gotten any sleep at all before returning to work in the morning.

He remembered how just hours before, or at least what seemed to him to be hours before, she had been talking about marriage. When she learned of his accident did she question, even for a moment, whether her plans of a life with him had been shattered? He thought about the teary exchange she must have shared with Stephanie as their moment of indiscretion was confessed, a result — Stephanie likely explained — of her own loneliness after a day spent in memory of her dead husband.

Then, to cap it all off, Jessica had gotten the ball rolling on the insurance claims. She'd probably called his parents as well. *God*, he thought to himself, *this if awful.*

It made him sick to think that his selfish, reckless actions could cause someone else pain. Jessica's presence there, beautiful and shaken, made him want to retreat into some dark hole. More than anything in that moment he wanted to disappear, to blink his eyes and be swept away to some mountain peak where he could scream and shout, kicking and clawing at himself, or just sit and look at the stars and no one would even know of his existence.

"Jessica, I'm so sorry," he said. "It isn't fair that you have to feel this way."

"What?" she asked, cooing like the dutiful partner she was. "It's ok. You gave us a scare but you're here. They'll release you in a few hours and then we can go home. I don't want you to worry about anything. Your parents are going to drive down tonight and we'll just go home and relax. We'll buy a bucket of ice cream and marathon through every James Bond we own until you feel better."

"I don't think we should see each other anymore."

"What?"

"I can't even express how grateful I am for what you've done, for taking care of everything and for being so amazing," he said, "but I think you should leave. Now."

"Charles?" she clutched his hand tighter but he pulled it away.

"I'm sorry Jess, I don't think we should see each other any more."

"Charles what is this about? Is this because of what I said last night? I'm sorry, I didn't mean to rush you, we don't have to talk about it right now."

"There's nothing to talk about. I'm very sorry but I think you should go."

"Charles you're not making any sense——," her voice paused, as though she was beginning to accept the finality of his tone. Until this point, her responses had been almost playful, as if guarding herself against a potential misunderstanding. Now she looked at him with fixed eyes, her voice low, her features set.

"I know," he said. "Now please, leave. I'm sorry to be like this. You deserve better, and I have no doubt that you'll find it."

"Charles, whatever I did I'm sorry."

"Don't apologize," he said. "You've done absolutely

nothing wrong. Now please, go."

"Charles," she said, her voice changing tone once more. "I love you. I'm not about to just walk out of your life without any explanation. You've been in an accident, you're confused. Let's just worry about getting you home and we can talk this all out when you're feeling better."

He said nothing because there was nothing to say. His expression was one of sadness, not malice or contempt. Cruelty was not his intention; he was not motivated by retaliation or a desire to punish or hurt her.

"I don't understand why you're doing this," she said, large tears welling up in her eyes. "Why are you saying these things?"

"There are no answers for what you're asking me," he said in a dull monotone. "I would like you to leave now. Let me know when you plan to get your things and I'll make sure to be out of the apartment."

"But, Charles. One bad night and you just want to end things? After all these years?"

"*One* year," he said. Quick. Short. The muscles tensing in his face. His voice had become something else entirely, almost animalistic as he punctuated those two short words. For a moment Jessica looked frightened, then angry, and then it was as though all emotion drained from her face like a faucet.

Charles rolled his body away from her to gaze out the window. It was sunny outside and from his vantage point one story off the ground he could see a playground full of children maybe two, three blocks away. He felt the bed shift as Jessica stood up. He heard the taps of her feet as she walked out the door and then the soft click as it swung shut behind her.

It was strange, but all affection he had felt for her was gone. Some dam within him, neglected and taken for granted, holding back every doubt and insecurity, had suddenly burst releasing a cascading torrent that washed everything away and left nothing behind.

A dull regret began to fill him as the sound of her steps diminished down the corridor, but it was not his heart that reached out after her. He felt a sense of rushing dread, as though he were standing at a cliff's edge waiting to jump. A voice inside him filled him with a fear that with her went his humanity, his hope, and whatever future he might hope to have. With each step she took, his resolution weakened. A cold, numbing sensation began spreading over him, soothing his tense muscles and quieting his troubled mind.

Charles suddenly felt tired — very tired indeed — and, slipping an arm beneath his head and pillow he closed his eyes and let himself fall into a deep, swallowing sleep.

CHAPTER ELEVEN

Jessica never attempted to change his mind. She was a smart, beautiful, remarkable woman, and rightfully saw little point in trying to convince a man to be with her. After a week or two, he came home one day to find her towel gone from the bathroom rack, the vase of flowers removed from the kitchen table, several empty drawers in his bedroom and a silver key waiting for him by the coffee maker. She had even washed the windows and vacuumed the floor before she left.

The first several days after returning home from the hospital were spent exactly as Jessica prescribed. The apartment soon became an 800 square-foot repository as he drifted in and out of sleep, drowning in a haze of pain killers. He was surrounded by empty Ben and Jerry's containers and burning through the 007 collection in chronological order, pausing only to use the restroom, masturbate, or slip downstairs to the corner market to buy more ice cream.

He woke up one afternoon around 2 p.m. feeling rotten inside and out. After throwing up and taking a violently cold shower he emerged from his apartment, blinking in the bright sunlight that had arrived with the first days of spring and spent the rest of the day walking around the city, breathing in the fresh air.

The next day he returned to work. Someone had adorned his cubicle with a "Welcome back Charles" banner, the letters hand-drawn with markers on copy paper like some last-minute grade school assignment. The ladies of the office had baked him cookies and the men took turns stopping by his desk to give him a pat on the back, which in each instance sent a wincing pain shooting from his damaged collarbone up into his temples.

He located a cleaning service online and overpaid a nice woman named Carla to cut through the layers of filth and discarded trash waiting for him at home. When he finally made it to the end of the day he opened his apartment door to find the space immaculate, each fixture gleaming and a lingering smell of minty-lemon freshness hanging in the air like a wispy cloud.

The most tedious element of his triumphant return to

society was slugging through the endless chain of phone calls from well-wishers. He had successfully dispatched his parents not long after being released from the hospital but that did not stop Jeff and Carol from "checking in" every night at 9:15. It was their perfect window to call as it gave them time for a solid 30-minute chat before the local news began but after NCIS or whatever crime procedural had aired on CBS that night.

Tyler and Trish stopped by early on and were then kind enough to leave him alone. Trish was apparently pregnant, an announcement they had been holding on to until after Devin's death-iversary. Apparently, in their minds, it was inappropriate to let any celebration of life interfere with the mourning of the dead. Charles couldn't help but think Devin would laugh at the attempts of decorum around his "sacred memory."

Tyler, of course, took the accident in a very masculine stride. He razzed Charles about not being able to hold his liquor and gifted him with the director's cut of *Gone in 60 Seconds*. "There's four minutes of extra footage," he had said, grinning ear-to-ear at the hilarious irony of his token of get-well-soon support. "But none of it is during the Angelina sex scene. I know right?"

Trish, for her part, simply shook her head in faux-disapproval of the boyish antics that so endeared Tyler to her, while repeating over and again with full sincerity how great it was to see that Charles was doing all right. They mentioned Jessica only once, as they were headed out the door.

"Jess?" Tyler had said, simply.

"Gone." Charles replied.

(pause)

"Well," Trish said, placing her hand gently on Charles' un-slung shoulder. "It's just so great to see that you're doing all right."

In lieu of a visit, Stephanie called him on the telephone not long after his return to work. They spoke for a little more than 10 minutes, with several long gaps in the conversation and almost all substantive topics left unaddressed. She asked if he was in pain. He replied that yes, he was, but he had the medicine to manage it.

"Daniel misses you," she said. "He keeps asking why you had to get hurt."

"Tell him I'll be better soon, and I'm sorry I can't visit."

She hung on the line a minute longer, clearly holding back thoughts she wanted to vocalize but couldn't find the words for.

"Are you sure you're all right Charles?" she asked. "I mean, really all right? Is there anything you need or anything I can do?"

"I'm fine Steph. Give my love to Daniel."

Within hardly any time at all, life was restored to its normal, monotonous pace. Days slipped into weeks and after about a month Charles ditched the sling and began, cautiously, re-instating the use of his arm. He started out small, taking short trips around the block on his bike while trying to keep the bulk of his weight on his good shoulder. Turning was complicated and at least twice impolite motorists had cut him off, forcing him to slam down on his breaks, pull over to the side of the road and collapse into a wincing heap on the curbside.

It continued to be an especially wet spring but the night of his accident looked to be the final snow of the year. The temperatures rose quickly, heralding the signs of colorful life creeping back into the city. Store fronts were now adorned with small bulbing flowers and in the mornings Charles could hear the birds cooing outside his window.

One particular Saturday morning, Charles awoke to a slight sweat as the unhindered rays of dawn beat down upon him. It had rained during the night, with the clouds breaking and the sun rising on dewy grass and bright blue skies. It was the kind of mythological morning from an American childhood where young boys build tree forts and chase each other with sticks.

Charles fixed a light breakfast of fresh fruit and toast. He showered and shaved and going to his closet to change he caught sight of the golf bag Tyler had left with him after the wedding. Despite having lived with Trish for some time, their possessions nonetheless doubled magically with the legitimization of their cohabitation and Tyler, in a gesture that said "don't worry, we'll still hang out all the time," had bequeathed his clubs to Charles for safekeeping.

They had been in the closet ever since. Such was life, it seemed, in that Charles' friends married wives while he went home to neglected toys.

Selecting a driver, Charles took a few practice swings to test his mobility, slowly at first but quickly at full speed. There was a stiffness in his muscle but the pain was gone. He grabbed the shirt nearest to him, slung the bag over his good shoulder and made for the door.

The driving range appeared to be completely empty and he worried as he approached the clubhouse that it was not yet open for the season. As he pulled his car — technically his mother's car since his Toyota was currently occupying a small square space in a lot somewhere — into the parking lot a 17-year-old working under the hood of a golf cart looked up and waved him over.

"If you're looking to play a round the back nine is a

swamp," he said.

"I was thinking I'd just hit a bucket at the range."

"Oh, no problem then. Just go ahead inside and grab some balls. You know your way around?"

"Yeah, thanks."

The range was mostly muddy and filled with the bumpy paths where mice had burrowed beneath the winter snow. But as the sun peaked over the trees Charles could see stalwart blades of spring grass lifting their heads from the muck to stretch their way back out into the spring air.

He teed up and shook out his shoulder, testing for any last warnings from his body that he should not proceed. Feeling nothing, he smoothed his arms back in a slow steady arch and struck the ball cautiously, sending it skipping along the ground in front of him.

"Well, that was just pathetic," he muttered to himself.

His next shot was better, sailing just shy of 75 yards before splashing down in the mudded lawn. After three or more swings he heard the familiar metallic ping as his club connected and the little white ball all but disappeared from view.

Watching it, likely the best hit he'd ever had, he thought back on his first attempt at golf. Tyler, the well-intentioned instructor, was barking instructions at him from behind as he continued to dig a sizeable hole between his legs.

"Keep your front arm straight. No, the front arm. But bend the other one. As you hit you want to follow through with your hips. Now pivot. PIVOT!"

For his part, Devin was mostly left alone to avoid the show. It was never clear why but Tyler had always taken to Charles as his student, leaving Devin to fail or succeed on his own volition. As Charles became visibly frustrated with Tyler's pestering, Devin graciously began asking questions of the master and diverting his attention away.

But now, as Charles stood alone at the top of a muddy hill, he had no need for a scapegoat as he had no teacher. He took a few more swings but, suddenly struck by and feeling uncomfortable in the silence around him, returned a half-empty bucket to the front desk with a five-dollar bill tucked beneath its base. Pulling out of the lot he gave a wave to the 17-year-old, who was now covered hand and face with motor oil.

Arriving home, he dropped the bag of clubs back into the closet and switched his sneakers for a pair of well-worn Steve Maddens before heading back out again. He checked that the windows were closed and latched, locked the door behind him and began walking down the street.

Traffic was light, and on every street bright smiling faces had heeded the call of spring to get outside and breathe. He was passed by joggers running with their dogs. He saw couples out for a walk swinging gleeful children between them and passed elderly city dwellers on patio furniture sipping drinks from large glasses dripping with condensation. On one quiet side street, a group of children were playing soccer and just as Charles passed a young boy with dark, curly hair passed a ball through the pair of shoes that served as goal posts, bringing an eruption of cheers from a scattering of onlookers.

He approached the library from the plaza, where a group of jugglers were practicing and the first stages of a drum circle were beginning to form. Passing the row of shops that make up the bottom level of the building's ramping arm, he could hear "Wait, Wait, Don't Tell Me" being broadcast from a pair of speakers and looked in for a moment at the glossy display of the comic book store, which was all but overflowing with the colorful images of super-human men battling evil for the sake of mankind.

Then he entered the library and walked down the atrium floor past the Hemingway Café, the English Garden and the Library Book Store. Above him hung the library's central piece of art, a giant human head made up of hundreds of paper butterflies and tiny books suspended from the ceiling. The installation hovered only a few feet from the curved staircase and as he climbed he wondered, as he often did, if the wires would support his weight if he were to dive out into the butterflies, gathering them up in his arms.

Reaching the top floor, he stopped once again at the center of the breezeway. The library interior seemed to him especially bathed in light, benefiting from an advantageous angle of the sun and the lowered expectations of a particularly colorless winter, which had finally given way to the birth of a new season.

From his perch, high in the air on a glass-lit cloud, Charles allowed his mind to wander. He saw himself standing with eyes closed, as though he were observing himself behind a crane-mounted camera, and watched as his body grew small as he pulled the camera back, drifting down onto the floor and moving backwards out of the library doors.

He saw the plaza outside, wrapped in green lawns and flowing fountains, then moved across the street passing cars and pedestrians as his mind left the city and climbed up into the mountains that guarded the horizon.

Charles imagined all the people around him, the entire population of a city with their individual tastes, talents and fears. Some would be enjoying a weekend off from work, others would be rubbing the sleep out of their eyes as they punched their timecard after a graveyard shift. Money would exchange hands, bones would be broken and property would be lost. He wondered how many children would be born today and how many people would die.

He thought about his friends – Devin, Stephanie, Tyler, Trish, even Jessica – how they always seemed to know what they wanted and how they did what they had to do to achieve it. Charles could almost hear that conversation with Devin around the fire, so many years ago, and how he had been so sure, fearless even, about marrying Stephanie and starting a family despite the cold reality of an all-but-certain death staring him in the face.

Charles asked himself what he wanted, what he *really* wanted. In his mind he saw Tyler and Trish sitting down to watch a movie with a bucket of popcorn and a blanket to cuddle under like a pair of horny teenagers. They would be surrounded by paint color swatches, having just spent 30 minutes debating the merits of two seemingly identical shades of blue for their unborn child's nursery.

Stephanie would be playing a game with her son on the living room floor. She would tickle him as he kicked and squirmed and then the two would pack up sandwiches and snacks for a picnic lunch at the park, where Daniel would make half a dozen new friends and Steph would banter with the other mothers about whose child was doing what at how many months.

He imagined Jessica sitting in a coffee shop somewhere in the city, wearing tight-fitting yoga pants, sipping a latte and holding a hardbound book in her hand. She would find a seat by the window where the light could dance across her skin and every man would be working up the nerve to speak to her.

Then Charles saw himself, weightless, relaxed with arms outstretched as he floated through the currents of the clear blue sky. The wind fluttered along his eyelids, cheeks and ears, tousling his hair and clothing while sending cool shivers down his spine.

There was a loud clap, followed by a high-pitched scream and the thunder of a hundred hurried footsteps. The sounds bounced off of every concrete pillar and every pane of glass, echoing through the open space on invisible waves.

Charles could feel himself slipping away, but he was conscious of a few things. First, there were several dull, blurry shapes frantically moving about around him. Second, his right arm was laid across a swath of sunlight that poured in from the windows. He could hear nothing but a muffled din that diminished with each moment and his mouth tasted strange and metallic. But from the flesh on the back of his outstretched right hand, bathed in sunlight, he felt the most profound sensation of warmth.

In downtown Salt Lake City, there is a beautiful library. It rises from the ground like a shining citadel of clear glass and angled concrete, overlooking the bustling traffic of University Avenue. On this day it was filled with blood and broken flesh.

Just inside the library's doors lay Charles' ruined body. His last thought, as a fuzzy, numbing darkness enveloped him, was that for as long as there were people still living who remembered him alive, he would be Mr. Charles Taggart, deceased April 13, 2014 at age 27.

ABOUT THE AUTHOR

Benjamin Wood is a journalist and writer who was born and raised in Huntsville, Utah and currently resides in Salt Lake City. He attended Utah State University, where he studied print journalism.

Benjamin's writing has appeared in the Utah Statesman, Utah CEO Magazine, The Deseret News and Entertainment Weekly. He has received awards for his writing from local and regional chapters of the Society of Professional Journalists as well as the Utah School Public Relations Association.

He can be found online at bjaminwood.wordpress.com or on twitter under his handle @BjaminWood.

Printed in Great Britain
by Amazon